D1292798

Home Fires Burning

690884

Home Fires Burning

By Dale Harris

PZ 4
H31347Ho

COMMUNITY COLLEGE OF ALLEGHENY COUNTY:
BOYCE CAMPUS
LIBRARY

THE MACMILLAN COMPANY, NEW YORK

Copyright © 1968 by Dale Harris

All rights reserved. No part of this book may be reproduced or transmitted in any form or by any means, electronic or mechanical, including photocopying, recording or by any information storage and retrieval system, without permission in writing from the Publisher.

Library of Congress Catalog Card Number: 68-19023

FIRST PRINTING

The Macmillan Company, New York
Collier-Macmillan Canada Ltd., Toronto, Ontario
Printed in the United States of America

For John and Susan Eyre

With Love

Home Fires Burning

One

A high-explosive bomb that did not explode fell into the back garden of Number Thirty-two early in the evening, and by dawn almost everyone in Jubilee Square had left.

The last ones to go were Number Five.

Just after the sun rose above the roofs on the opposite side of the Square, the old woman who owned Number Five came out onto the front step and stood against the doorjamb, sunning herself.

With eyes closed and head tilted upward, she remained there for several minutes, a rinsed-out milk bottle in the crook of her arm, until a fly settled on her face and roused her.

Quickly but carefully she placed the bottle at the side of the step, reached inside the doorway, and in one swift movement brought from the dark passageway a tall, hairless man. Once outside, he instinctively drew himself next to her, bone against bone, whimpering with fear of the daylight and plucking nervously at her arm while she turned from him to lock the door behind them. The moment she finished with the door he pressed himself to her, and when she pulled him along the pavement she had to keep him at a stiff arm's length to prevent herself from being tripped up.

Just after they turned the corner into Cluster Street, a warden in a red helmet stepped in front of them.

"All right—be quick about it. We don't have all day. They're waiting for you at the shelter."

The wrinkled man began to whimper.

"There's a good chap. You just go along with her. She'll take care of you all right."

But he drew himself closer to his mother and plucked at the white scarf around his neck.

"Stop that," she said, and giving him a sudden jerk, pulled him along with her down Cluster Street without saying a word to the warden.

"The Grine Street shelter," the warden called out after them. "Tell them you're the last lot from here."

He turned his attention to sealing off the entrance to the Square with a coil of red-flagged rope.

Three weeks after it had fallen, the bomb was dismantled and carted off by sappers. The coil of rope stretched out across the entrance to the Square was wound up and taken away.

But no one came back.

Night after night the bombers roared overhead. One evening the docks caught it. A sugar warehouse burned for two days, turning the sky the color of honey for miles around. A few nights later it was the city. An incendiary smashed through the roof of St. Paul's and blazed up before the main altar. Department shops in Regent Street became rubble; and nightclubs in Leicester Square, churches in the Strand, factories in Bermondsey. All over London—in East Ham, in Highbury, in Shepherds Bush, in Camberwell—small houses were burned black or blown suddenly into dust.

Inside the Square, the brass letter boxes turned green and black. Some days a moving van would come to pick up furniture, boxes of clothes, carpets in long, sagging rolls, and carry them off to the suburbs or the country;

2

but otherwise no one came there, and the empty milk bottles outside Number Five remained uncollected. The washing left hurriedly behind by the woman in Number Twelve grew heavy with soot. Stray cats, pressing themselves against doors that had all been locked from the outside, sent leaves flying when the guns in the park nearby frightened them into taking shelter. And all the time the wind moved about the pavement, carrying scraps of refuse, blowing it through the iron railings, depositing it against the basement walls.

Then one day just before dawn a land mine fell in the Square. The white silk parachute that bore it floated calmly down, but with every cord stretched taut from the silk to the steel beneath. A few feet above the roofs the parachute slackened. A long, slow rippling moved across it, and it billowed about like white steam. Suddenly it crumpled and was gone. A burst of flame swept away the fog and the grime, and in an instant the Square was alive with wind.

By the time the fire engines arrived, smoke and dust and grit swarmed in the air. One side of Number Eleven crashed downward, and a hot hail of sparks gushed out. All over the Square, dark shapes of timber and brick surged hissing among the flames, until just before noon, when the roof of Number Fourteen caved in and the blaze was finally smothered in water.

In the ashen afternoon, wisps of smoke crept along the ground while water slobbered down the rubble. The three neat sides that had enclosed the Square were gone, and the gray light spilled over into the jagged spaces. In some places the outside walls were ripped down, leaving the upper floors, still full of furniture, suspended in midair. Long strips of wallpaper curled across the

3

cornice at Number Twenty-six. By the splintered doorway of Thirty-one the top half of a small plaster statue lay inverted inside a porcelain washing basin. High up on the single wall of Number Ten, a tap dripped slowly upon a mirror that hung ten feet below.

Only a few stumps of blackened brick house, insides burned out but walls intact, stuck up above the rubble: Numbers Six, Eight, and, directly across from them, Number Five, taller than the rest. All the others were down, and everything was changed.

Two

Week after week Oxley lay on his back in complete darkness, swathed rigid. He dreamed endlessly, awake and asleep, unable to tell the difference. After a time he began to hear. An airplane. Footfalls, coming close, going away. A woman calling to him in a voice he knew, but through an immense lethargy from which he would not rouse himself. Then he recognized the smell—a chemist's shop, a dispensary, a bedside—and he felt his body begin to loosen.

At last, while unknown hands moved among his bandages, he heard with great distinctness a man's voice saying, "I think it's going to hold all right, don't you, sir?" and after that he knew what had happened, and the dreaming stopped.

The morning they took the gauze from his eyes, he looked down at the nurse working on his body and followed the dim shape of her while she spread putty-colored ointment over his stomach with a small flexible trowel, placed lint upon the area, and then covered it with fresh bandages. He had felt her working at him every morning, starting at his head and passing down to his feet, section by section. She bound up his belly and began on the next section. He continued to watch her for a few minutes, but the sight of her fingers there at his thighs, the blunt trowel, the feel of the wet, cold oint-

5

ment upon his flesh, made him turn sick, and he kept his eyes closed until she had moved away from his bedside.

A week later, after most of the fever had left him, the doctor gave him a hand mirror to see how well the job had been done, but he turned his face aside and refused to look.

Two days after Oxley was allowed out of bed, the Colonel, an elderly, pink-faced man with long, unmilitary hair, sent for him to tell him that he was being discharged the following morning.

The desk before which Oxley sat was wide and covered by glass. The top was bare except for a highly polished shellcase mounted upon an ebony base, and a brass ashtray with the word "YPRES" scratched into it. The Colonel leaned on the desk. Under his hands there was a single manila folder.

The Colonel said, "I realize it's a bit quick, but, you see, it's the space problem again. We really need the space. If times were normal, of course, you'd stay on here for, well, at least two weeks more. Convalescing and getting on your feet again properly."

While the man spoke, Oxley heard sounds from outside the windows, voices from the convalescent officers' area. He had left the others drinking lemonade in the smoky mess; sitting in the draughty back garden that looked over the sea to the Isle of Wight and the gray convoys creeping out to the Atlantic; visiting the tight-faced girl in tweeds who usually asked, "A nice 'tec story for you this time, perhaps?" when she took back the library books through a hole in one of the basement walls; playing solitaire on splintery tables in the recreation room run by a Salvation Army woman who sang "Roll Out the Barrel" under her breath all day long and sometimes made tea.

6

He indicated that he did not care for one of the cigarettes the Colonel had taken from a pocket in his white coat.

"But, even so, you know, there's not really much more we can do for you." The Colonel looked haphazardly at the contents of the folder. "There will, of course, be a pension. Full disability." He waited. "Any idea of what you'll do? There are lots of things a young fellow can do these days. It's not like the last one, you know, with millions killed and gassed and not much to show for it when it was all over, either. You'll go back to Cambridge now, will you?"

"I'll have to see what it's like first before making up my mind. Look around me, sir." Oxley closed his eyes for a moment. "I'll have to see. But not Cambridge, sir: I think it's past that now."

After lunch he tried to put through a call to Salisbury, but there was a delay of almost four hours, and by the time he got hold of a free line his mother had gone off for her evening at the W.V.S. canteen. He spoke instead to Doris, the bow-legged girl from Amesbury who had come to them in the summer before the war when he was getting ready to go up to the university. He left a message that he would be home the following afternoon. But because the connection was poor, the line was full of intrusive, strange whispers, and he had to repeat his words several times before he could make her understand.

That evening he saw himself for the first time. Deliberately. When the ward was quiet and all the other patients were asleep he went into the bathroom where—in the way he had learned during the past two days—he cleaned his teeth without once looking at his stiff-feeling lips in the mirror above the basin. Afterward, with his gaze still averted, he stepped back a couple of paces as if to prepare himself for a long leap forward, and then turned his eyes to the mirror.

It was the same face. He saw that instantly. The face he had always known. Now with the youth flayed out of it, he realized for the first time that all the gentleness of feature he had never been aware of before had been turned into sudden age. Cheek, chin, nose, brow, stripped down of their soft flesh, were almost at one with the hard shape of the bone beneath. A thin covering of patched and waxy skin stretched across his skull.

The skin was strangely glossy, the surface permanently unfocused. It was like a photograph, the image fixed forever, in which he had moved his head, so that everything, both shape and color, was smudged. The forehead high in the place where the once light-brown hair had been eaten away; the blue eyes, watery and scarlet-veined now, set deeper and darker between the protruding cheekbones below and the shiny knobs for eyebrows above; the colorless mouth, stretched like old elastic, pushed a little to one side and upward, so that henceforth, no matter what the pain, half his face would be smiling. And upon it all, the white creases at the eyes and at the mouth and the nostrils, as if the skin had been tightened up somewhere at the back of his head; the dark streak at the temple; the deep red channels at the neck.

Then, beneath his pajamas, his discolored body in the glare of the unshaded light bulb.

He switched off the light and went back to his high antiseptic bed halfway down the ward. He lay awake for a long time. Every now and then—pushed sleepless by a crowd of thoughts—he raised his head from the pillow to watch the night nurse. She was reading *Fur and Feather* under a green-shaded lamp, and she shifted the position

8

of her feet, as if with impatience, beneath the steel table. As hard as he could, he pinched into his thighs. When at last he fell asleep his fingers were fast around them.

The ceremony in the morning was very simple. The Colonel had taken off his white coat before Oxley came into the office. There were a few words of sympathy, hesitant and embarrassed, as though the old man had no idea about what to say to someone leaving the hospital under circumstances of this kind.

"Good luck in civvy street, young fellow," he said finally in a jocular way. Then, after a moment in which he seemed not to know what to do with his hands, he put them behind his back and smiled at Oxley, dismissing him.

Oxley picked up his papers from the desk. The single sheet on top released him from the hospital; the foolscap file, from his commission. There was nothing else, no equipment, no personal gear apart from the clothes he was wearing, and they had been sent from a nearby regiment that same morning.

After saying good-bye to the Colonel and to a bearded captain who had come into the office without any warning halfway through the farewell ceremony and stared intently at his face, Oxley left.

Oxley heard them talking through the closed door. He shoved the papers into the pocket of his raincoat and ran, hobbling slightly, out of the building.

Three

He stood on the pavement outside Salisbury Station, uncertain for a few moments about which way to take for the Cathedral Close.

The train pulled out noisily and thrust through the afternoon on its way to Basingstoke, Woking, and London, where everything came to a stop.

The sounds of the town rose to him: bicycle bells, motor engines, a loud voice here and there breaking the surface of street noise. Straight before him, toward the High Street, the familiar people could be seen: farmers in corduroys and caps with the peak to one side, bicyclists, women toting shopping baskets, a few old men. But also now, wherever he looked, there were soldiers. They stood about on street corners, propped themselves against walls and shop windows, walked in groups along the roadway—shabby and bored and ogling at the girls going by—filling in the time before the picture palaces opened and the fish and chip shops and then the pubs. There was khaki everywhere: it seemed to him as though Salisbury Plain had spilled out all its troops upon the streets of the town so that they and the civilians could wait together for the invasion that might come now at any time.

He did not go in the direction of the crowded High Street but turned instead to the right at the corner pub, on one of whose walls someone had painted a large V.

He walked down Mill Road, past the row of semide-tached houses where schoolteachers and clerks lived behind stained-glass doors and lacy curtains. There was no one about. Across the river the old meadow was cut up now into vegetable gardens for the war effort; the Cathedral spire looked odd above it.

Mill Road was quiet. Every now and then the sound of traffic from the High Street absorbed the soft plash of the river. A fresh-faced girl of about seventeen in a chocolate-colored school uniform went slowly past him on a bicycle. She turned round to look at something, and he immediately lowered his head. Out of the corner of his eye he saw that she hadn't noticed him. He watched her long pigtail flap across her shoulders as she rode off.

Nearing the house as slowly as he could: the book shop with the complete Hazlitt in thirty-four volumes still in the window; The Wool Basket, showing off bright angora jersies, Fair Isle tammies, and, shoved to one side like something unpleasant, the photograph of a sailor wearing a balaclava—all under a large "Not for Sale" sign; the archway; then at last the Cathedral, and the immense silence of the Close.

The place was insulated from the rest of the town; it was all stillness, even when things moved there. The black birds that rose from a hedge as he went by seemed unnatural and lifeless; with their slow mechanical-sounding whirr and their sharp flutter upward they were like expensive toys.

Doris opened the door just enough to show her blunt nose to the daylight. A stillness more intense than that of the Close seemed to lie waiting for him in the hallway. Going inside the house, he felt his skin begin to prickle. To his surprise he found that there were beads of sweat

11

on his forehead. He wondered how the sweat could penetrate the new, alien skin. In the last numbed days he had thought of it as dead, something borrowed, like the pelt of a strange animal. His hand went to his forehead while Doris stood back in the doorway. The skin was alive, part of him. He felt along the sharp ridges at his brow. His entire face was clammy. Sweat trickled into his eyes. He tried to wipe his face with his hands.

Doris began to follow him down the hall, waiting for his coat. He couldn't bring himself to look directly at her, to see more of her than her hands and, above them, her white cuffs, starched and dazzling against the shadowy wall. He heard her say something. The sweat stung his eyes. With his face to one side he undid his raincoat and tried to think of something to say in return. He pushed the raincoat toward her. Finally he said, "Doris," and then, having nothing more to add, he tried to smile in her direction. But as he smiled the muscles in his cheeks started to twitch violently; the skin around his mouth stiffened, pulled back, resisted. All at once he was overcome by the fear that his face was about to come apart, would any second split wide open. He put his hands up to his cheeks and mouth and stood there holding himself in. His face, his eyes, burned. He wanted to cry out. He wanted to run from the house with his hands around his head.

He heard Doris nervously speak his name, and his grip relaxed. But he did not reply. He turned his back to the girl, and without dropping his hands he pretended to wipe his brow. Swiftly and covertly, not thinking of what he was doing, seeking only the reassurance of his fingertips, he felt his face all over. He used tiny, delicate movements, like a blind man trying to visualize a stranger. As he touched his mouth he remembered that the smile was already there.

He went quickly down the hall, wanting to get as far away from Doris as possible, confused about where he was, despite the familiar objects that surrounded him. He stopped, and from the gloom where the fanlight didn't reach he looked about him: at the oak chest, the Delft bowl, the convex mirror with a splayed gilt eagle on top, the pastel portrait of his great-aunt MacGrimmon. He realized that he would have to relearn them, would have to remember where everything was as if he had never seen them before. He ran his hand along the rim of the bowl, and at last reached slowly toward the door to the sitting room, where his mother waited.

Just as he was about to grasp the doorknob it turned by itself, and the door opened. He tried to step back from it, but the movement caught him off guard, and the door struck him painfully against the shoulder. In the confusion he was aware of his mother's presence before he actually saw her. He heard her draw in her breath with surprise at finding him so close, felt the heat of her blood and the pressure of her arms when she reached out for him. As she took him to her, embraced him tightly, he realized that she had done so without trying to see what he looked like. She pressed her head to his chest and stroked his arms. She did not raise her head, but kept it on his chest, breathing hard, thrusting herself upon him so that he stood there supporting her. Then, hardly withdrawing her body from his, she began to guide him through the doorway. Pulling him along with her she said, "My baby, my baby." Fast in her grip, with nearly all her weight against him, locked together, stumbling awkwardly, they moved into the sitting room. As they did so he was overwhelmed by the feeling that he had done something to her that she would never forgive him for.

By the time they were inside, had left Doris by herself

13

in the hallway with his raincoat bundled in her arms like laundry, his mother was weeping. Her head was still down, and she stroked his arms with fierce solicitude. She seemed endowed with extraordinary strength. She drove herself into him as though she wanted to crush her grief out of existence. He felt the convulsions of her body pass through him while she wept. Held tight against her, he was forced to share in her anguish. Flushed, distracted, hearing the noises in her throat, feeling them come to life upon his chest, he could hardly separate his own emotions from hers. A scalding heat fixed itself at his eyes. He thought he must weep like a child, fall limp and sobbing into her strong embrace. But the tears did not come. And though at the sound of her voice he sobbed, it was only once, like an echo. The fear passed out of him. He was immeasurably tired. He locked his knees to brace himself against the weight of her body and felt the gold brooch she wore digging into him, her nails upon the flesh of his arms, the toe of her shoe pressing down on his crippled foot.

Her tears came to an end. She was silent. She pointed toward the bow window, where the small table was set for tea and the kettle steamed. She let go of his arms and balanced herself. He felt the weight of her body drop away from him.

"Are you all right?" he asked, and she replied, "Yes, yes," distractedly, put her hand up toward his face as if she meant to touch him, and then let it fall to her side.

As she went to the table she said, "Come and sit down. Come and sit next to me." She was dry-eyed, and very pale. The strength seemed to have left her.

He said, "Mother, will you be all right?"

She drew her chair into the table. "Please, dear, sit down. You haven't to worry. There's nothing to be upset about. You're home now. Everything will be the way you remember it. Please come and sit. You have your life before you."

She laid a starched napkin on her lap. She began to talk again, and blinking once as if to steady herself, she turned her eyes fully upon him.

And there at her tea table, with the light from the big curved window directly behind her, he felt the first stab of bitterness inside him when her voice stumbled, stopped, went out of control, like someone falling off a curb, and she turned her eyes to the tea things below her.

When she recovered and was able to look at him again, he was reminded of school and the way their games master used to address them after losing a match. It was as though he were watching something already half forgotten.

For a while she seemed not to know what she was doing, pouring tea endlessly even when the pot was empty of all but a final dribble, playing with tongs and sugar and milk. Her cup grated against the saucer; she broke one dry biscuit, dabbed up the crumbs with her forefinger and put them in her mouth; and all the time she talked.

She seemed to be afraid of leaving him alone with himself, of giving him time to think. He tried to tell her that he was tired, but she pressed more tea upon him. He began to speak about the hospital, to find some way of apologizing for what he had become, but even before he said more than a few words he saw fear in her face and he stopped. She wanted only to distract him with her voice, with talk: of trains in wartime, food these days, a nice fire in his bedroom, evacuees, Uncle Percy, Cambridge, all his books, the eggs she had hoarded for his homecoming during the weeks gone by, the W.V.S. canteen, wartime sacrifices, something more about evacuees.

He recoiled from her as she sought to draw him back into the world of home. While she spoke he realized that the surgeon's skin pulled him away forever into another life.

By then it was already evening. He saw that her loose brown dress had grown larger, that it was fading imperceptibly into the sky as the light behind her drained away. She began to gather the dusk into her body. Only the gold brooch fastened just below her collar caught a gleam from the tea things between them.

She rang the hand bell. It was shaped like a lady in a crinoline, and the brass skirt clicked harshly on the table when she put it down.

"We need more water. I know how much you like your tea," she said to him, as though they had been apart for years and she remembered everything about him nevertheless. "We're having a blackberry and apple pie in your honor. That was always your favorite, even as a little boy."

Immense in the twilight, she bit into another of the dry biscuits.

The room was full of the dark sky. "Doris," she called out when the door opened, "we need more water. You can draw the blackout curtains now, as well." The tone of authority he remembered so vividly from the past was back in her voice as she addressed the maid. She moved her chair a little way out of the window to allow Doris to pass behind. "Doris, don't you think it's nice to have Mr. Oxley home again?"

"Oh, it is, ma'am." She sounded scared when she spoke, and she did not look in his direction. "It's very nice to see him again. Very nice, ma'am, very nice," she repeated, her hands full of black cloth that grated along its runners when she pulled it.

Doris opened the door, and a crack of light shone into the room, a thin wedge of brightness right through the beige flowers of the carpet. Across the room, from the direction of the kitchen, there came an indistinct sound of voices.

"Doris," his mother said as the girl was feeling along the wall for the light switch, "how's Mrs. Clatley's son today?"

Doris stopped moving. "Much better, Mrs. Oxley. He was in the dumps earlier—a bit restless he was with his stomach this morning—but he's got his appetite back again now."

Mrs. Oxley addressed her son in the dark. Her voice sounded very strong. Doris kept still, as though waiting for her to finish. "Mrs. Clatley's an evacuee from London. They'd been out on Boscombe Road before, but the woman there fell ill and couldn't cope any longer—so of course I said we'd take them in. There's the whole of this vast house and nobody to fill it. It was while you were away." She sounded bitter. "I felt cut off." Her resentment surprised him. "I said yes, there and then. We have to do something in times like these; we have to make an effort. They're up in Doris' quarters. Houses like this were built for a big staff. Evacuees would be no trouble at all, I said. In any case, it's wartime. You can't let people of that sort just take their chances. As long as they're clean: I don't see that one shouldn't demand at least that much of people, even in wartime. There have been some appalling incidents with evacuees. But she does look after the son very well." He heard her touch her cup. "Doris," she said, "do you have the switch?"

The darkness of the room was broken up into amber pools of light. As Doris closed the door behind her he rose from his chair. His mother had shrunk in the illumination. The gold brooch was somewhere among the folds of her brown dress and the tea things were in the shadows.

"Mother," he said in a voice that was full of breath, "I'm going to my room. I'm very tired. I'm sorry."

He turned on his heel.

"Seven o'clock dinner as usual, dear," she began. "Sharp, because of the extra work these days for Doris and . . . ," but as he hobbled away from her across the room her voice crumbled, and without looking round he heard something, a spoon, a knife, the sugar tongs, clatter on the table top and fall dully to the carpet among the beige flowers.

He didn't touch any of the light switches but climbed the stairs in darkness, feeling with his hand along the banister rail until he had made his way through the upstairs hallway to the door of his old room. Once inside he crossed to the window and peered out into the darkness of the town. There was nothing to be seen, not a movement, not a glimmer in the blackout. The cinemas, the pubs, were full, the alleyways were lined with soldiers and their girls, but on the outside of the town there was only the safety of night. He felt an odd sense of excitement when he thought of what the darkness held. Through the window he could hear the sound of an airplane moving over the heart of the country, leaving the room silent.

He drew the curtains and fell on his black bed. There was no need to turn on the lights; it was all there, he knew: the life before. His mother would have seen that nothing was changed. He kept his face, new, alien, pressed down hard against the counterpane. After a while he felt its familiar raised pattern of acanthus leaves biting into his cheek.

18

For a long time he lay quite still, his mind unaware of anything but the knowledge that he would carry with him forever like a withered limb the memory of the past.

Around him in darkness were his possessions: clothes, tennis racquet, books, the battered trunk with continental hotel stickers all over it, the stamp album from his schooldays, piles of magazines—*Film Fun, Hotspur;* then, later, *Lilliput*, the *Spectator*, *Horizon*—every magazine he'd ever bought. He remembered the hours he used to spend arranging what he owned, making a place for them on shelves, in odd corners, in the cupboards, packing them away carefully, fitting them into his room as though he were filing evidence.

He sat up on the bed, staring into the darkness. He thought of his fat, stuffed room. In his head he made lists of the objects around him, everything he could remember. As he spoke the names to himself he realized that he never wanted to see them again. Complete sets of cigarette cards in albums: the Kings and Queens of England, Famous Racing Cars, Great Moments in Science. The Gramophone records. Mark Hambourg, plum label; Alfred Cortot, red label; Kathleen Long, on Decca; Lili Kraus on Parlophone-Odeon. He thought of the girl at Murdoch's slipping a free package of needles in with the records. Letters in bundles, from the family, from friends. Picture postcards: Cleethorpes, Harrogate, Dieppe. Pictures of girls. Photos of Kate, thirty different poses on one sheet. A sequence of faces, all Kate's. He remembered the way she ran through the expressions: drawing up the corners of her mouth, pulling the corners down, closing her eyes, pursing her lips, a tragic look with eyebrows knitted, an angry look with teeth bared, showing her tongue daintily, clapping a hand over her mouth, breaking into laughter, laughing hard, unable to stop—so that the last five poses were all the same.

19

She had tried to burn the photographs only a week later. When he and she were lying on the floor by the gas fire in his room looking them over and giggling, Kate suddenly burst into tears, snatched the sheet from his hand and flung it against the incandescent grille. He had retrieved it quickly enough, though an edge was singed and he burned his finger reaching for it. He put the photographs carefully among the pages of his *Times* atlas, out of her way. When he stretched out again on the floor by her side, the burned finger in his mouth, she held his chin and kissed him and told him she didn't want him to think of her like that, a clown, and he put his hands under her arms and held her to him.

He thought of the photographs he had saved then, and he thought of the letter that arrived at the hospital from her. Against his wishes she had replied anyway to the curt note he'd written the week before, designed to end all contact between them. He had been ashamed at the sight of her letter. He had torn it up, without reading it, as soon as he recognized the handwriting on the envelope, and had flushed it down the lavatory the day before he was discharged. He had stood there bent over the bowl for a long time, inhaling the acrid smell, listening to the rusty pipes knocking and rattling as he watched the water splash, settle, turn clear.

The hands of the clock in his room glowed at a quarter to seven. He made his way downstairs past everything he once owned. He did not go back into the sitting room. He walked out to the garden, trying to collect himself. A half moon broke the clouds. He turned his face toward the far wall of the garden and the muffled town beyond it. The night air swirled around him while his eyes became adjusted to the darkness. After a time he was able to make out the vague shapes of the garden and the outlines of the path that led across the lawn to the little summerhouse. He walked toward it, feeling calmer.

The wooden step stiffened under his feet, and the door of the summerhouse scraped open upon the black interior.

"Hello there," a voice called from inside the room. "Shut the door—it's damp." A woman's voice, dry and flaky, like old paint.

There was a sound of whimpering at the back of the room, and the voice, turned now toward it, said, "Stop that!" and there was silence until he spoke out into the blackness.

"Who are you? What are you doing in here?" During the pause that followed, he took a step into the room.

"Shut the door," the voice said again. "You'll let all the night air in."

He did not move.

Small, old-woman steps came toward him, a sleeve brushed across his hand, and the door behind him squeaked shut. The footsteps tapped away over the bare floorboards to the far end of the room. "Be still when I tell you," the voice said into the back of the room.

There was a sound of wicker stretching as she sat down. Her voice turned to him again. "There's a chair right next to you. It's by the door. You might as well take a pew, you know, what with your leg and all."

"Who are you?" he said. "What business have you got in here?"

"Us? Oh, we like it here, that's all." Her arm rustled in the darkness like something made of paper, and there was the small clink of glass beads. "Nice and quiet. We come in here every night so as to get out of that house. We sit in here nice and quiet till it's time to eat."

21

"What do you mean about my leg?" he asked, still standing in front of the closed door.

"Oh, don't worry about that—we know what's up, we do. We know all about you. We saw you coming along the front garden from our window in that house. Knew who you was the moment we saw you down there. We heard all about it from Doris, so we knew straightaway." She clicked her jaws. "No mistaking you, I'd say, once you've been told about it."

"Who are you?"

He struck a match and held it before him. But he could see nothing except the flame pushing into the darkness.

"Here," she said quickly, "put that out—and sharp, too! There's no safe blackout in this place, just them old shutters. We don't want none of your silliness here. That's not what we come out to the country for."

He shook away the flame and dropped the match to the floor.

"Evacuees," she went on, rustling her sleeves, "that's what. Cooped upstairs next to Doris, while old pin eyes sits down there in all her glory. We know her, all right—her and her wartime sacrifices. If Doris had any gumption she'd give her what-for one of these days. Wartime sacrifices, indeed! I'd wartime sacrifice her, I would." Her voice became lower. "We know her all right, don't we, Ray-Ray?"

He heard the sound of boots scraping into the floorboards.

"Here," she said, "stop that. Say hello to him, Ray-Ray, and keep yourself still when I tell you. We'll be eating shortly. Something nice and tasty for a change, I hope. Yes, that's better."

She was silent for a moment, and he heard the sound of her beads in the darkness like insects striking against a windowpane. "Come to think of it," she said quickly, "you'll be late for your supper, won't you? She eats at seven, right on the dot. Right on the stroke of seven, she eats. I know that well enough because we don't get a morsel till Doris finishes running around after her. She'll give you hell if you're late, won't she?"

He sat down in the chair by the side of the door. Without thinking, he felt with his fingertips along the pebbled surface of his neck. When he realized what he was doing he began, gently and rhythmically, to stroke his skin, slowly exploring the new surface, its unevenness, its contours.

"She'll give you hell, won't she?" the woman asked again.

"No." He spoke in as harsh a tone as he could force through his stiff lips. "No, she won't." His hands moved over his roughened cheek.

"Come on now—you know what she's like, the same as I do. 'Clatley,' she says to me the first day—but only once, mind you. I soon let her know I've got a handle to my name. 'Oxley,' I says right back to her. Well, 'Clatley,' she says to me when she shows me over the house that time, 'young Mr. Oxley, him in these here photographs . . .'" But the old voice stopped, and the sleeve rustled out in his direction through the darkness. "It *is* your mother, I suppose," she said reflectively, and then added abruptly, "you feeling sorry for yourself?" She waited. "Are you?"

"Yes," and there was no trace of harshness in his voice when he spoke. "I am." He put his elbows upon his thighs.

"Yes," she said, "I expect you are. Well, it'll just put acid in your stomach, so you might as well learn to make the best of a bad job. You're not the answer to a maiden's prayer. But that sort of stuff doesn't last for

23

long—and what are you left with then, eh? There *is* worse, you know."

"Worse? What difference does it make? There isn't anything worse for me, is there?"

"It's not like you was incapable, is it? You know what's what, well enough. Know how to eat for yourself and use the W.C. and so forth."

"Yes," and the words spurted out of him through the black room, "but that isn't all, is it? What about the rest?"

"You're lucky to have that much. You don't have to have someone over you night and day to keep you from fiddling with the dog and getting into trouble with the gas stove and the bread knife."

She waited before going on and when she spoke again her voice was low and insubstantial.

"There's some," she said, "as can't do anything for themselves. They have to have a person by their side all the time. And in the end it don't really matter to them. It's like they was an animal you kept in the house for companionship. Something with blood in it. You're not that bad off, are you, now?"

"I wish I were." He spoke with anger in his voice.

At the far end of the room a chair moved. He heard her getting to her feet.

"You wish you was what?" she said.

The darkness, the disembodied sounds, loosened his tongue. He directed his words into the black space before him. "Incapable that way. Out of it altogether. The trouble is, I know what's happening, don't I?"

"Well," she said, very still, "you're not incapable. And be grateful for it. What you do's in your own hands. You're independent. Don't wish the other on yourself."

24

He listened to her footsteps. It sounded as though she was walking around her chair.

"Out of it altogether?" she continued. "Where's the sense in that sort of talk? Life sticks, no matter how you feel about it."

He heard her pulling a chair in his direction.

When she stopped she said, "Being angry like you are is daft. Who you got it in for?"

"Why do they think it's such an achievement, the doctors, to save you no matter what? They patch you up so that you can last out your time. What for? What do they imagine you can do? Start again as though you've been in storage?"

He pushed his chair back hard against the wall and got up.

"Here," she said, "don't go off in a huff. Don't mind me."

"I'm sorry," he said. "It's easy to be angry in the dark."

"You don't want to brood about yourself."

He made a gesture toward the door and, beyond it, the house at the end of the garden. "It's not just for myself. I see the effect I have on people. I can't blame them. I walk around like a testimonial to medical skill, don't I? It's hard to get past that. You can see the workmanship a mile off. All done by hand." He leaned back against the door and began to pull at his neck. "There was a girl in the train this afternoon, sitting opposite me, reading. It was funny, the way she reacted. After I got into the carriage she sat there for half an hour trying to keep her eyes on her book. In the end she had to give up. She went and stood in the corridor until she saw I was getting out. I wanted to hide myself. I keep wondering what it can be like for people who know me. The people I knew before. I feel I ought to apologize to them. I feel

25

as if I've swindled them somehow. Gone away one person and come back another. I'm sorry for them. Everyone I've seen wants to be kind, but they don't know what to do about it."

The old woman came toward him. "Why don't you go away for a holiday? It'll take you out of yourself a bit."

There was a sound of whimpering at the back of the room. "Ray-Ray?" She went to her son.

"Is he all right?" Oxley asked.

"Yes!" she called out with vehemence. "Yes, he is!" Then she said quietly, "Not much longer now, ducky, and we'll be having something nice and warm to eat. Here now—don't snivel." He heard her fumbling in the darkness. "All right now—blow hard, hard as ever you can."

For several minutes there was silence in the room. Then the old woman spoke again. "He was calmer at home. Knew where he was. Knew what to expect. But I couldn't take him back to the raids. It's funny," she said, "the house is still standing. After all that. They tell me it's the only one you can see when you look along Cluster Street." Once again she walked toward him. "You ought to get away from here. You could stay there. You could move in for a while. Number Five Jubilee. Give yourself a change. London's not a bad place, bombs or no bombs. You can have a bit of fun there. Not like the country. I wouldn't charge you. Tit for tat. Me and Ray-Ray here and you there. Unless you'd like to offer something, of course. You wouldn't know a soul in that part, either, would you? You could get used to things if you had a bit of time to work with. It might need fixing up a little, though. Well, think about it." She clicked her jaws. "Now you be off to your food. The sooner you tuck in over there, the sooner we do. You're late as it is."

26

She laughed as she heard him move.

"See if she don't give you hell, like I said. She knows what I think of her. Go on, look sharp."

He opened the door. Outside, the moon was gone from among the clouds, and the room was stirred by a breeze.

"Can I help you across to the house?" he said above the squeaking noise of the door. "It's very dark now. I know the way."

"Just you get a move on, so's we can eat soon, that's all. We'll follow quick enough. Don't you have no fear about that."

Four

Waterloo was crowded. Servicemen with duffel bags, civilians with suitcases and little bundles. Men and women arriving, waiting, departing. Oxley looked around at the porters and ticket collectors, the kiosk attendants behind the "No Cigarettes" signs. He went for tea to the buffet, where the solitary spoon was fixed to the counter by a chain and rested, between stirrings, in a mug of steadily darkening water.

Then, with his attaché case at his feet and his raincoat slung over his shoulder, he stood among the smoke and litter of the station reading down the "Lodgings" column of the *Advertiser*.

Above his head a sign from a previous age—"Taxis to Victoria: Boat-Trains for Paris and the Continent" —was almost obliterated by grime, its arrow leading nowhere now but to a bus queue and fading posters: "Horlicks Soothes." "Own Your Own Home Through Abbey." "Sanatogen for Lifelong Youth."

When he finished reading, he picked up his case and walked out toward the city.

A boy in a brown jersey that almost hid his short trousers accosted him and asked for a penny. Noise surrounded him—train whistles, the thrust of escaping, scalding steam. He turned his head to one side as he walked on, trying to avoid the boy.

The boy kept beside him. "Got a penny, mister? For the lav."

28

Soldiers swearing, regularly, monotonously, without interest. Babies being carried off crying to the country. A pair of girls in pink rayon turbans giggling together at the side entrance.

"Mister—" the boy wiped a sleeve across his wet nose—"a penny won't hurt you. It's for the lav, honest it is. I've got to go bad. Number two, honest, I've got to do number two." Oxley gave the boy a penny and walked on quickly. He heard the boy's voice calling after him, "Stingy, stingy." And then, in the side streets behind the station, everything thinned away into quietness and the movement of an occasional, anonymous passerby.

He knocked on the door of a house at the end of a blind alley. The house was wedged between a brick wall and a cat's meat shop. Opposite the entrance to the alley he saw the ruins of a pub. Its sign, "The Bull and the Gate," was still fixed above the gaping doorway; through the doorway he saw a pile of debris, covered in lumps of dry, powdery earth. On the pavement outside, a public urinal—square, olive-green, elaborately patterned with cast-iron lilies—still functioned, undamaged, spitting and gurgling.

Oxley watched it through the alley entrance while he waited on the front step of the narrow house for someone to answer his knock. He turned to face the blue enamel plate with "No Hawkers" spelled out on it as soon as he heard someone at the door.

He saw the woman's apron first. It was magenta, and its pocket bulged. Then the head, metal curlers sticking out all over it.

"Oh"—she put a plump hand to the curlers—"yes, can I do something for you?"

He pointed to the "Lodgers" sign in the front window.

"Oh, it's that."

She stepped back inside the doorway and looked him

over very slowly. She stared at him, his face, his neck, without flinching. He saw her appraising his clothes, his attaché case.

"Yes," she said, "come in," and she took the raincoat off his arm and the case from his hand before he knew what she was doing.

She steered him through a dim passageway into the front parlor. It was as full of colors and as crowded as the inside of a needlework box. When she sat down on the sofa her swansdown slippers did not quite touch the carpet. She put his case and raincoat next to her as if she wanted to be ready to snatch them up at a second's notice.

He took a chair on the other side of the room under a cage of budgerigars. They chirped wildly above his head as soon as the clock began to chime the hour. He felt as though the crowded room were moving in to smother him, with its birds, antimacassars, fringed velvet curtaining, wax fruit under a glass dome, a scene of the fleet at Hong Kong done in colored beads, a pair of copper horseshoes with enameled shamrocks.

She watched him closely. "I'm house proud," she said. "I've got an eye for comfort. You look the type who's used to a nice home life." She waited, as though she expected him to confirm what she had said.

He tried to avoid her eyes. He looked away from her and nervously stroked the plush armrest of his chair.

She watched him. "It's good furniture, isn't it? The bed-sitter you're after," she said, "that's a treat, too. Very nicely done. Convenient." She looked at him from under heavy lids. "Like to go and see it? It's upstairs." She took a soiled paper bag from her apron pocket and fished out a sweet. With a small, dainty gesture she laid it inside her mouth.

30

"Fancy a jelly baby?" she said when the sweet was gone.

He shook his head.

"It's not easy having a sweet tooth these days, is it? Things are getting really bad, aren't they? Don't you think I'm right?"

Again she seemed to wait for him to discuss her remarks. He moved his head up and down in a vague way.

"I'm lucky," she went on after a minute. "One of my gentlemen here knows where to get sweets from. He's very clever that way. He's got the cheek of the devil. How long do you think you'll be staying?" She removed her apron while she spoke. Her print skirt was as tight across her hips as the label on a beer bottle. "I don't really like to do it for less than a month. Less than that would hardly be worth it. Getting to know people, all their habits and ways properly, it takes a bit of time—though it's true, none of the gentlemen stay long these days. The war's got everyone on the move, hasn't it?" She looked at her hands. "Have you come far?"

"No," he said, "not far. A month will be all right. I'm in London to look around. For a house. I should think a month will be all right. Would you like me to pay you now?"

She moved through her furniture as though she were playing musical chairs and took a seat nearer his.

"Well, I must say you don't waste much time making up your mind, do you?" She looked up at the cage of budgerigars. "Nice things, aren't they? Ever so lovey-dovey. Aren't you?" she said to the birds. "Aren't you, you little beggars, eh?" She turned back to Oxley. "Yes, all right, so long as it's a month, Mr.—?" But as if to reassure him, she went on immediately, "I'm Milly Swizzick. Mrs., that is. He's in the army. Pioneer Corps.

31

Probably digging a lavatory in the middle of a field somewhere right this minute. It had to be the Pioneers. His health was never too good." She began to remove the curlers while she listened for his name. "Health's important, isn't it?" she said. "What was your name?"

"Oxley, my name's Oxley." He reached into his inside pocket. "I'll pay for the month now."

She let her hands fall into her lap. "Well, maybe you'd best see it first. We're a very friendly lot here, you know. I like to keep a friendly house. I like to think of all my gentlemen as guests. People you can trust. There's two others, both of them above you. Perhaps we ought to take a look at the room before you pay, don't you think so? It's very quiet here. No kids, or anything like that. Shall we go up together and have a gander at it? How do you spell your name?"

While he told her, she stood up and placed her hand against the side of the birdcage. She drew a black curtain over the cage while her eyes darted about his face. "You from London?" she asked.

Her inquisitive eyes made him nervous. "No," he said.

"Been in any air raids?"

He shook his head.

"Oh, well. I just wondered." She changed the subject as if disconcerted by his silences. "I think even the budgies ought to have their privacy, don't you?" She set the covered birdcage swinging on its brass hook and laughed. "Nice weather today, don't you think? It makes a change." She moved before him into the passageway. "I'll go up first."

Oxley picked up his raincoat and case.

"Christ!" she said suddenly. "Gawd help us!"

A tall man had appeared at the foot of the stairs. He

stood chuckling against her side with one arm around her waist, while she rubbed the bottom edge of her corset. "Saucy thing you are, Freddy." She disengaged herself with a plump wriggle. A large sausage curl had fallen like a broken spring over her forehead and began to unwind itself down to her eyebrows. "A pinch in time saves nine, you know." He laughed into her face. He stopped when he caught sight of Oxley in the parlor doorway. "Hello, hello, hello."

"Oh," she pushed the curl back into her hair, "our new lodger, name of Oxley. Mr. Oxley, this is Mr. Straker, Freddy Straker, one of my gentlemen."

"Hello, matie," Freddy Straker said, squaring his shoulders. "Welcome to Milly Swizzick's home away from home." He looked at the attaché case, the raincoat. He caught Oxley's eye. "Milly here will soon fix you up. A real cheerful soul." He turned back to the woman and laughed. "That's right, isn't it? Well, I'll see you later on, Mil. Cheerio, all."

She closed the front door behind him and beckoned to Oxley to follow her upward.

"No cooking up here, of course," she said, slightly out of breath when they were almost on the landing of the first floor. The stairs smelled of boiled greens. "No electric plates, gas rings, Primus stoves, and so forth. Once you allow that, I always say—" she paused for breath and placed another jelly baby on her tongue—"you can expect anything." She pushed the door open and went inside.

The room was a shabby relative of the parlor downstairs. On the marbled mantelpiece there was a limp peacock feather stuck into a port glass. She waited for him to look around the room properly, to take in the heavy china pitcher and basin, the matching chamber pot, the inlaid teak cabinet, the double bed with brass knobs at the corners, the mirror in which he could see himself from where he stood by the door. The pitcher, basin, and pot were all embellished with a view of a seaside pier at night.

She stood quietly by, as if waiting for him to examine every object in the room, to appreciate all the details that went to make a home away from home: the rocking chair with a not-quite-clean ashtray on its seat, the gray lamp shade suspended from a wall bracket and the light cord that stretched from it across the lumpy pink eiderdown. There was also a picture postcard of cherubs playing with flowers among clouds. Part of the plaster had fallen away from the ceiling, leaving a jagged pattern of slats in the whitewash above their heads.

"Nice, isn't it? I don't like my gentlemen to come into a bare room." She stood in front of the teak cabinet. "All my rooms are properly furnished. The stair carpet goes all the way to the top of the house—which is more than you can say of most places."

He saw her clay-colored hair and her soft, fleshy back reflected in the mirror just below the image of his face. He moved to a place at the side of the door from which he could no longer see directly into the mirror, but he kept his eyes upon the woman.

"Nice, isn't it?" she said again. She flopped onto the far edge of the bed and began to bounce up and down. "Nice, eh?" She waited for his words of approval. "Very soft and comfortable. See? See how soft it is? I think you'll like it very much. A comfortable bed's important if you've got trouble with your back, isn't it? Maybe you'll stay longer than a month, eh? After all, if you don't mind me taking the liberty, it does seem a bit daft getting into a house these days, what with everything so uncertain. And think of the inconvenience. Men don't like that sort of thing much, do they? You'll have a lot less trouble taking a room like this, you know. Are you going to be in London long?"

The jelly baby was gone from her discolored tongue.

"I'm looking around," he said.

"Come up for a job, have you?"

Her curiosity oppressed him. He began to sweat as she stared at him.

"Everything'll be taken care of here," she went on. "No worries about furniture or cleaning. Everything available here except the cooking. And men don't like to fuss with that anyway, do they? You come from a large family?"

Again he shook his head.

She looked up at the ceiling. "Blast from when The Bull caught it." She pointed to the slats. "Quite safe. I couldn't get a plasterer to come and do it, and, anyway, what's the use at a time like this? You've got to be thankful for anything nowadays, haven't you? Here today and gone tomorrow. I'm a fatalist when it comes to the bombs. Either your number's on one of them, or it's not." She looked at him closely. "Been in the army, have you? See any action?"

Oxley reached for his wallet. He shifted his feet and rubbed his damp palms against the leather. "I think a house is really what I need," he stammered out the first thing that came into his head, "for business reasons. It's for business. The room will do till then. It's very nice. Thank you. I'll pay you now. I have to go out."

She got up from the bed. Her foot kicked the chamber pot. She smoothed out her dress. The light-cord had fallen off the eiderdown and it trailed across the floor by the bed.

He was standing before the mirror again, and he could see his face above her hair and one soft round shoulder.

"I have to go out now and find out about the house."
He opened his wallet.

The smile came off her face. "All right"—her voice
was high and thin—"one month. In advance. Eight quid,
flat. There's no extras. Satisfactory, I trust."

He handed her the money across the wide bed,
stretching his arm out all the way over the pink eiderdown and the cord, which she had returned to its orig-
inal position. He stepped backward to the door. They
were still in the mirror together.

"The key to the front door and this room—which I
strongly advise you to keep locked at all times for your
own benefit—they're both on a nail against the side of
the hall stand downstairs."

When he opened the street door he heard her call
down the stairs after him, "No cooking, mind you. I'm
firm about that."

Five

"All the way, please."

"Cluster Street?" the conductress said in a flat Midlands voice. When she had punched his ticket she added, "It's a long way from Waterloo, chum," as though apologizing for the tenpenny fare. "A long ride on these utility buses. Still," she moved down the bus, "nothing's easy these days, is it?"

A soldier wearing steel-rimmed glasses and carrying a khaki towel came and sat next to him. At Charing Cross the bus filled up completely. It began to get very warm. People stood packed together in the aisle; someone wheezed asthmatically over Oxley's head. Sitting all the way down front, he could see the other passengers reflected in a strip of the glass behind the driver's seat where part of the protective gauze had been torn away. Below it there was a notice showing a man in a bowler hat wagging his finger at someone peeling the gauze off a bus window:

> *"Hold on, young fellow—not so fast!*
> *That stuff is there in case of blast!"*

As they neared Paddington the bus began to empty. The soldier got off at the station. In the window to Oxley's right a diamond-shaped viewhole had been cut from the gauze. He watched a girl in trousers kissing a sailor at the entrance to the station. A bulging duffel bag was propped against the wall next to them.

37

When the conductress called out: "Changing drivers, chum. Hold tight for Cluster Street," Oxley turned round to find the bus empty. He sat there completely alone, shivering in the chill that spread through the bus.

Outside the unprotected glass diamond the girl was still in the sailor's arms. His hands were clenched together just above the base of her spine. A small boy ate fish and chips from a newspaper and stood nearby watching. Between mouthfuls he pursed up his lips as though he was making derisive sucking noises at the couple. The sailor grinned at the boy and kissed the girl again. A pair of Red Caps walked slowly out of the station and made for the Salvation Army hotel on the corner, where a newspaper vendor was waving the early edition of *The Star*. A dribble of people formed a queue for cigarettes near the goods entrance, and a Dutch officer went by with a nurse on each arm. The nurses were laughing, and the Dutchman waved his hands about excitedly, showing a mouthful of gold teeth when he spoke.

A thin-faced girl came down the empty aisle and stood over Oxley as the bus began to ease forward again. Nobody else got on.

He held out his tenpenny ticket. "I'm going to Cluster Street."

"All right, mate"—she sat down on the seat across the aisle from him—"nearly there. Four more stops and that's it." She began to put packs of bus tickets into her wooden holder. He watched as she eased open the tight springs that held the tickets in place, and then let them snap shut. After a while she looked up at him. "Lucky you brought your mac, mate. The wireless said cold and rainy tonight, and it's already starting to spit down. You don't know where you are when it's like this, do you?"

She snapped the last pack of tickets into place and then began to read from a pocket book.

After the bus swung around into Cluster Street he saw that the pavements were turning glossy. He was surprised by the emptiness of the streets.

He watched her read. "Not too many people around here these days," he said, staring straight ahead as he spoke. "I thought, in London, there'd be more people about."

She raised her eyes from the book. The cover showed a girl running across the drawbridge of a castle and looking back over her shoulder wih a terrified expression. "The only chance I get for a bit of a read." She held up the book for him to see; it was *The Confessions of Maria Savage*. "It's good. I read fast when I can sit down and concentrate. People? There's plenty. The trouble is, it's only quiet round here at this time of day. The rest of the time you're on your feet every minute. I hate doing the night shift on this route."

She put her finger in her place in the book and stood up. She peered through the glass diamond. "Well, we're here. Cluster Street Underground. Watch how you go now, mate."

An air raid warden leaned against the pillar-box on the corner, smoking a home-rolled cigarette and letting the ash drop indifferently on his jacket. "Jubilee Square?" He turned his head to the north. "Up that way." He spat the butt end on the pavement. "It copped a fine bloody load, I can tell you. Not much left of it now."

Farther along, an old woman came out of The Cluster Arms. A man's tweed cap was fastened to her head by a long steel hatpin, and she carried a jug of beer with the midday dog-racing results on top of it. A card nailed to the boarded-up window of a fish and chip shop said: "Frying Tuesday, Friday, Saturday Only. Bring Your Own

Paper." The smell of stale fat hung in the air. Outside the Cluster Empire there was a poster for a film about an Eastern princess. She wore diaphanous pajamas. Behind her there was an erupting volcano and a crowd of Indians. The washed-out pink stucco of the cinema was chipped and flaked all over, and the neon sign was smashed by bomb blast. The whole street had the seedy, neglected appearance of old clothes, old food, old faces. He stopped to look in the window of a rubber-goods shop. Among the trusses and syringes, the packets of Staminoids ("for nerves and energy"), the elastic bandages ("made to your special needs"), the tubes of jelly contraceptives and boxes of foam tablets, he saw that pride of place went to the books, each one wrapped carefully in cellophane as if guaranteed sterile: *New Memoirs of Casanova, White Slavery in Our Time, Fulfillment in Wedlock, The Whip and the Rod.* Four Polish soldiers stood next to him reading out the titles to one another in a guttural accent. After a while they went into a restaurant called The Allies, where a middle-aged woman stood at the door singing to herself and knitting.

He came to a sharp halt. A hundred yards or so ahead of him the road opened out to the sky. He walked toward it as quickly as his leg allowed—past The Marquis of Fotheringay, a window full of service badges and insignia, a doctor's office in what had once been a shop, a shiny new siren that dominated the entire street.

A gust of wind blew across the open area, and for a moment he stood shivering inside his raincoat. Then he walked into the Square.

There was little debris. Everything large and removable had been taken away, and only the smallest pieces of smashed brick were left. Red and orange, glistening from the recent shower, they lay scattered all over the ground like part of the landscape. Three house shapes were still standing in the leveled Square. They were blackened by fire, and the roofs and top floors of two of them had been sliced off. The remaining one, the one he had come to see, was firm against the sky. It was propped up on either side by huge timbers, themselves blackened and charred, salvaged from another bomb wreck nearby. Nailed over the roof, the doorway, and the slim windows, a skin of housing felt was stretched tight. A figure five was painted on the wall to the left of the doorway.

The canal lay behind the house. He saw that its banks were fat with shiny green growth. For a while he stood looking at the stray bits of refuse thrown from back gardens—tins, food peelings, clothing—and then went back to the house.

He leaned against it with his hand resting on the crisp-baked brick, and he stared across at the canal. There was no one about. The house, the Square seemed completely isolated. He felt a sense of great relief as he looked around him. It was getting dark as he walked slowly back across the Square toward Cluster Street. He was covered in sweat.

Just before he turned the corner on his way back to the underground station, he stopped for a moment to look around at the Square and saw the painted five quite clearly.

It was several minutes before he realized how many people there were about. Then the smell of frying fat came at him, he heard voices and the sound of piano-playing from inside The Marquis of Fotheringay and The Cluster Arms, felt men, women, moving around him in the night, realized by the time he was at the station that in the blackout Cluster Street had suddenly come alive.

Six

He woke up again, shivering a little from the cold.

He had been dreaming. He was in the middle of an empty room and people were tiptoeing round and round in single file. He kept his head down on his chest all the time, but he could still see their feet. He felt the ground shake as they went past.

The eiderdown had slipped off the bed. He pulled it up across his body, thinking that tomorrow morning he'd be gone, he'd be in the house, alone. He began falling backward into darkness and warmth. Beyond the alley a train moved across the viaduct in the direction of Waterloo. Voices on the stairs. On the floorboards.

A woman laughed. He sat upright in bed, as wide awake as though he had never been asleep. The cord from the lamp brushed against the side of his head. He jerked it away from him. Something heavy fell on the floor above. He looked up, as if trying to penetrate the blackness. He heard the sound of breaking glass: a jar, a bottle, a light bulb. The woman's voice said loudly, "Oh Christ, no!" Milly Swizzick's voice. She laughed again, and a man made shushing noises.

Oxley sat there rigid in the darkness, listening. Above him a piece of furniture was being moved, and a man said, "Easy does it. Easy." For several minutes there was no sound, only his heart beating. Then he heard something being pushed against the wall. Then silence.

He waited, hoping the noises would start again, sweating, straining to hear. But the house was completely hushed.

A long time after, tensed and dry-mouthed, he eased himself down among the bedclothes with his hands around his thighs. He thought of the woman up there beyond his head, imagined her plump buttocks, the soft flesh shaking, slammed hard against a wall. He began drifting off into sleep, thinking about her, visualized her upstairs with the man. She began to turn into other people. He had a slow chaotic vision: a nurse moving her legs beneath a table set for tea, Kate laughing, men and women feeling their way around in the dark, changing places with one another, all of them moving—silent, effortless, supple, like something under water—through the house in Jubilee Square.

But he could not fall asleep. He listened for the woman's voice. A train went by in fits and starts. There was a gust of air behind the blackout curtains, and he heard the scatter of rain on the window. At last the rain stopped. He was bent nearly double in bed, holding his thighs, straining to hear the woman through the distant irregular sounds of the night.

"Heavy, this one."

He must have dozed off again.

They were talking. He couldn't tell where the voices came from. Something was being dragged up the stairs. His hands were stiff. He loosened the grip on his flesh. Pins and needles ran through one of his arms. He wanted to move it about to ease the discomfort, but he didn't dare for fear of making a noise, for fear of being heard, of not hearing. The people—Milly Swizzick, the man—were talking too softly. He caught only disconnected phrases—"wake the house," "lovely item," "red-handed, red-handed"—and then the woman in a congested voice, like the sound of a wireless turned down too far, suddenly singing the line, "Stop your tick-e-ling, Jock."

They seemed to be carrying things up the stairs. The rain was at the window again. Drifting back into sleep, he thought of the morning, of the devastated Square and its single house; the blackout along Cluster Street; bodies moving unseen, with only their feet visible every so often in the beam of someone's torch; people, strangers, warmth, soft flesh in the darkness—always in the darkness.

He heard them on the stairs once again, heard the woman right outside his door whispering: "You've got the cheek of the bloody devil. Ask him yourself. He'll be gone in the morning, anyway. It's too late," heard her easing her way downstairs and the sound of shoes, one, then the other, dropping upon the bomb-damaged floor above his head.

Seven

There was the man again. On the corner outside the tobacconist's now, with his face turned away; the back view was enough to identify him.

A few days before, Oxley had heard the conductress say, "Nice afternoon. But rain tonight, don't you think?" to somebody else going beyond Paddington. When he got up, the other passenger was already jumping off the platform even though the bus still moved along at full speed, and he caught a glimpse of blue checked suiting, of greasy hair that lifted for a moment and then fell around the man's face in small, black curves. A few minutes later he saw him again, under the awning of a jellied-eel stand on the opposite side of Cluster Street. Farther north he realized that the man was keeping pace with him, a few steps behind. He watched the stranger's reflection moving steadily across the window of Hollywood Shoes, of Smalley's Bikes and Meccanos, of the Home and Colonial. Later, just before he pushed the front door shut, he turned around and saw that the man was standing at the entrance to the Square, looking down Cluster Street, with his back to the house and the canal.

The tobacconist peered at Oxley from the rear of the shop. In one hand he carried a box of drawing pins and in the other several envelopes and cards and pieces of paper, all with writing on them. "No, mate, sorry. Haven't seen a cigarette for days."

The shop looked half-abandoned. Dust lay everywhere. The shelves had nothing on them but a few stone bottles of ink and a sign that advertised, "Brock's Fireworks for the Coronation." On the counter there were only empty jars and some out-of-date magazines: *Red Letter*, *Tit-Bits*, *Beano*. A wrinkled poster on the wall behind the cash register showed an aviatrix in white leather overalls smoking a cigarette and smiling.

Oxley looked out of the window. The corner was empty. He could see no one in the street, either.

"Live up this way, do you?"

Oxley shook his head.

"Work here, do you? If you was to keep coming in maybe I could put you on my list of regulars."

"No," Oxley said, "I don't know how long I'll be around."

As he left the shop the man came from behind the counter and followed him into the street.

Oxley examined the street again. There was no one in sight.

The tobacconist opened the glass case on the wall outside the shop. He proceeded to rearrange the cards and envelopes and pieces of paper on display there, making room for the new ones he had brought out with him.

Oxley looked over the man's shoulder at the handwritten messages, the notices, the advertisements. In the last weeks he had stopped to examine display cases like this whenever he came across them. "Nice Dudley pram for sale," he read now. "Back room to let in Bister Street, private." "Pen friends all types wanted." "By appointment, Miss Whipp." The tobacconist locked the case up again, and Oxley saw the stranger's reflection in the glass.

He made for the Square without turning round. He

tried to walk calmly, but his pace quickened involuntarily, and he felt his hobble become more pronounced.

A few days ago when he first realized there was someone following him he had been gripped by terror, almost gave way to it by running down a side street. Seeing the stranger then, he believed himself cornered. His only thought was somehow to escape, to disappear. But he kept on walking, controlled himself. A man with greasy hair in a blue suit, the streaked reflection of someone he did not know, was enough to make him afraid. He had cut himself off from everything; he did not want to be claimed again.

He wondered now if the stranger would once again follow him all the way to the Square. At The Three Fiddlers, where a charwoman had propped the door open with a pail that smelled of carbolic, he saw the familiar reflection in the engraved glass. He knew then that he would have to confront him. Across the empty, open Square he forced himself to slow down. This time he did not enter the front door. He walked round the side, underneath the huge salvaged timbers that shored everything up, to the back of the house. He stood against the wall that faced the thick water of the canal and the fat weeds beginning to push their way toward the house. He heard the crunch of footsteps on the smashed brick.

The man came round the corner. Oxley saw a hand stretched out toward him, listened to the voice, jovial and vaguely familiar, saying, "What a coincidence. It's really funny, eh? Remember me? Freddy Straker—," saw the man pushing his hair out of his eyes and then waiting. "Milly Swizzick's," the man added. "Upstairs from you. She introduced us your first day—remember?"

"What do you want with me?"

"Freddy Straker's the name."

"You've been following me. All the way from Waterloo. I watched you behind me the entire afternoon. And a couple of days ago. What do you mean, coincidence? You've been trailing me."

Oxley stood against the wall and looked directly at Freddy Straker.

But the man's eyes did not hold still. They kept moving, over Oxley's face, to the right, to the left.

"Really lovely," Freddy said, jerking his head round at the canal.

"What are you after?"

"Don't be like that, chum." He squared his shoulders and lowered his eyes. "No harm meant."

"Who sent you? What do you mean, lovely?"

"Sent me? No one sent me. Just give me a minute. I ask you, mate, do I look like the sort that wouldn't be open with you? We don't want to get going on the wrong foot, do we? Everything friendly and aboveboard—that's all I want. See?"

The moving, crafty eyes met Oxley's and remained still. There was something in his manner, shifty as well as cocky, that made Oxley lose his fear.

Oxley said, "What are you after?"

Freddy Straker looked round at the canal again. "I'm interested in you. Want to do you a favor. Both of us. We both stand to gain. Look here, why don't we go inside and I'll tell you what's up."

"What possible favor could you do for me? Why should you be interested in me?"

Freddy nodded toward the wall with its sealed-up windows, its obliterated back door. "The house, mainly," he said.

"The house?"

"It's really lovely. Ideal. Why don't we go inside and I'll tell you what I was thinking of?"

"No. Tell me here."

"Jesus bleeding Christ! How the hell can anyone talk business like this? In the broad daylight?" Freddy waved his hands about.

Oxley turned away from him and for a minute he faced the house: it would only be his till the war ended and the buildings went up around it again, hiding the canal, joining the Square to the end of Cluster Street; then the old woman would come back to claim it once more.

He watched the movement of Freddy Straker's white nostrils twitching with impatience, and the hair, like bat's wings, falling across his face whenever he jerked his head. "Talk business? What for?"

"Good profit for both of us, that's what for."

"Come inside," Oxley said abruptly, and turned to-ward the opening at the front of the house.

They sat, in the downstairs parlor with folding doors, on old leather chairs with round seats and high, uncom-fortable backs. The leather squeaked beneath them every time they moved. In the middle of the ceiling the electric light fixture was bare. The five curling iron rods where glass shades had once hung looked like a grape-stalk picked clean.

"Nice," Freddy said, "very nice indeed. You could really make something out of all this."

Oxley had placed a wire-handled roadman's lantern on a piano stool between them; it was the only source of light in the room, red glass around a crescent of orange flame. Freddy looked things over with great care. The windows, sealed from the outside, reflected the room, smoky-red, except at the top, where two panes were missing.

"I'm leaving those covered up till things get better," Oxley said, watching him.

Beneath the windows all the old woman's aspidistras

and ferns were pushed together into one thick, matted clump that filled the entire room with the smell of damp green growth.

"Yes," Freddy said, "well, it saves you putting the blackout up every night, don't it? Only a couple of them missing, and all that damage outside! Well, it just shows you." He leaned forward. "Shows you, most of all, it's a lucky house. I like it."

"Every other window in the place was blown out. This is the only room with the windows still in it. The cupboards upstairs are full of broken glass."

"Well, I like it," Freddy said. "Mind if I have a quick look at the rest while I'm here?"

"What was the business you wanted to talk about? Was that the reason you've been following me around?"

"Yes. Have a fag?" He drew out a heavy silver case, and Oxley took one. "Balkan Sobranie. Hard to come by unless you know how. I tell you—it's like this: Milly says to me, 'He wants to buy a house. A house? What's he want with a house at a time like this? Up to something funny, if you ask me,' she says, and, well, I thought so myself. Only saw you once, of course, but you didn't act natural to me. You looked like you might have the coppers on your mind. 'He's up to something,' she says, 'mark my words'; so I thought to myself, All right, we'll see. So I followed you out here, and you did look nervous, I'll have to say that." He waited and looked modestly down at his shoes as though expecting Oxley to congratulate him. When Oxley said nothing he went on, a little less confidently, "You give yourself away. Not natural enough. I mean, to me you do. I've got a sharp eye."

"What's your guess, then? You think I look nervous. Why?"

"I reckon you got something on your mind, mate."

"And you want to cash in on it somehow? Are you thinking of blackmail? Is that what you meant by a business offer? I don't think much of it as an offer. You can't go very far on just being suspicious."

"No, no," Freddy said, looking uncomfortable. "You got me the wrong way. I just thought you might be interested in having a go with a little business. It's a good time for it. You look like someone worth going partners with. I followed you to strike up a friendship, see? Well, then, I have a look at the house and I studies the whole thing and I says to myself, Hello, hello, hello, it's *very* nice. Smashing, in fact. Beautiful location." Once again he smiled broadly, and then said, "I still don't know what your line is exactly, though I've got my thoughts about it. But what I'm thinking is how well we could get on together, you and me. This house, you could make it into a real gold mine—but then, maybe I'm not telling you anything new, eh?" He saw the frown on Oxley's face and waited. "That's my offer," he added.

"The woman, Mrs. Swizzick, where does she come into this?"

"Oh, don't worry about *her*, she's got nothing to do with it. She's just crumpet. Gets randy with her old man away, so you have to oblige when you've got the time. Trouble with Milly is she's all mouth. Got nothing up here, has Milly." He tapped his forehead and then passed his hand across his hair. He laughed. "Not that high up, her talent."

Oxley remained silent. He got up from the chair and stood over Freddy Straker, then tapped the cigarette on his tight knucklebone. Inside the clenched fist, his palm was hot and wet. "What's the line you're in?"

Freddy cleared his throat. "I'll be direct with you. Can't ask for more, can you, now? It's merchandising I'm in. Not too large a scale, mind you, but the real

51

thing, strictly the best, de luxe trade only." He put the cigarette case back into an inside pocket and smiled. "Good-tasting fags, eh? Imported special for me from America. Well, a lot of it's tin stuff—peaches, pineapple, fruit cocktail, asparagus tips. Then there's coconut. And mayonnaise, chocolate boxes, olive oil, ham, Christmas crackers—all of it's quality goods. Only the best. Perfume as well. Beautiful stuff it is, too, I can tell you." It was a swift patter, like a barker at a sideshow. He took out his handkerchief when he came to the end of his list and flicked it a couple of times before putting it to his nose. "I can also manage a ton or two of coal—all nuts, no dust—for those who want it. Though I don't much like that line myself." He opened his eyes wide. "That's being honest with you now, isn't it? And what's yours?"

Oxley frowned. "My what?"

"Line of business. Fair's fair. Trust," he said, "complete trust. I'd say we got to have that above all, right from the start. Don't you think so? Right now I need you, and I expect it'll end up with you needing me just as bad. This house—"

He looked at Freddy Straker, with his soiled handkerchief crumpled in the top pocket of his suit, talking of chocolates with colored paper round each one and fancy bottles of scent—"None of that muck, that Californian Poppy stuff." All the small luxuries were gone now. Meals were mainly on the order of cabbage and mashed potatoes, with a sausage, and maybe Yorkshire pudding on Sundays if there was ever an egg to spare. Day after day he had eaten food like that near Waterloo and on Cluster Street. Everything Freddy talked about belonged to prewar. For most people, it was all gone for the duration. But Freddy's stuff wasn't meant for most people, for places like Waterloo and Cluster Street. "The West End," Freddy Straker was saying confidentially, "Earl's

52

Court, and out that way—that sort pays good money for fancy items, you know. If we can only get in touch with the type." And this house would be Freddy's storeroom, piled high with tins and bottles and boxes. There would be callers and arrangements for payment and fresh supplies. There would also be lowered voices and packets under overcoats, inside prams, at the bottom of carrier bags.

". . . Well," Freddy was saying, "I ask you, did you ever see anything more ideal? What a location! After dark it'll be as easy as winking. One, two, and Bob's your uncle. We'll be rich in no time. What about it, eh?" He laughed and then suddenly stopped. "What's that? The door," he whispered, "the door. Someone's outside."

It was a slow, hard knocking.

"Stay here. I'll be back." Oxley closed the parlor door firmly behind him and felt his way into the lightless hall, past Mrs. Clatley's stuffed weasel under a cracked glass dome next to the umbrellas.

"Good day, mister."

The light took him by surprise. Although the afternoon was gray, the color of the room remained before his eyes like a dull red haze. Then he saw the caller, a small man with bloodshot cheeks and a lantern jaw rough with what looked like a week's white and ginger stubble.

"Trigg's the name, mister," the caller said. "You're in me district. I happen to notice someone took the felt off the front door and come over to find out what's up. Everything all right, I suppose? Thought I'd just have a look-see. How's your blackout?" He put on his helmet. It was dented on one side, and the white paint was flaking off. "You ain't busy, are you? Work a night shift?"

Oxley shook his head. "Everything's fine. What do you want?"

"Me? *I* don't want nothing, mister—I thought *you*

53

might. You're new, ain't you? I used to know the people what lived here before. Nice lot, the old lady and her boy. They all right? You a relative or something like that?" The man turned and coughed drily. After he was finished, he put his hand to his mouth in a deferential gesture. "Excuse me," he said. "This cough'll be the death of me yet. Here—you wouldn't have any tea around, would you? Terrible attacks of phlegm I get. Nice hot cuppa would set me up like new. Terrible, this phlegm."

"No, I don't. I eat everything out."

"Your blackout's all right, then? We can't take no chances after what happened here already, can we? This place, you know, it's exposed, what with all the other houses gone. They say it sticks out from up there something horrible, especially in the moonlight. You want to make sure you have your stirrup pump and your sand and your water ready if Jerry comes over again. Water's running all right, I suppose? And the electric's back on?"

"Yes, everything's running perfectly. And nothing could show through the felt, could it?"

"That's right. Well, you can't be too sure, can you, now? Haven't had any trouble from rats, have you? They say the canal's swarming with 'em these days. Nasty, rotten things, ain't they? If there's one thing gives me the creeps, it's rats. All covered in fleas and nits, every inch of them. Big black whoppers. Take a bite out of your bum the size of a cabbage head. Haven't seen none, have you?"

"No, I haven't. The house is in good shape now. I'll be careful to show no lights."

"Yes. Well, all right, then." The warden shuffled his feet. "Why don't you come down to the post and have your gas mask checked when you got a bit of time on your hands? There's usually something going on, game of cards or something." He coughed, this time behind his fingers. "By the way—as long as I'm here—you don't happen to have any fags in the house, do you? I'm cleaned right out at the moment."

"No, I can't help you. I've none myself. Afternoon."

"I see. Well, no offense meant, I'm sure. Here to help and that sort of thing. Sorry to trouble you." He touched his helmet. "Afternoon, mister."

Oxley pushed the bolt across the door and stood there in the dark by the side of the umbrellas and the glassed-in weasel. He felt safe again inside the darkened house. But he would have to make sure he got no more calls, was never thought of as part of the neighborhood, was left in place in the isolated house.

He went back to Freddy Straker and the red haze of the roadman's lamp.

"Who was that, for Christ's sake?" Freddy spoke in a rasping whisper.

"No one in particular. The local warden."

"It put the wind up me for a moment. What's he after?"

"Nothing," Oxley said. "I don't think he wanted anything much. He said it was the blackout. I really think he wanted to talk—mainly about black rats big enough to take a bite out of your arse."

"What the hell for?"

"No harm in him. Just an old skate, but I don't think he'll come back."

"They're a lot of nosy buggers, if you ask me. Tell him to hop it next time."

Oxley sat on the chair opposite Freddy, with his legs stretched out all the way and his hands hard upon his thighs. "Straker," he said, "you want to use this house for your stuff—"

"Merchandise." Freddy's interruption was emphatic. "Black market goods, in any case. That's what you want it for, isn't it?"

Freddy broke in. "Look at it this way: they're all luxury items." He spoke quickly, and as he spoke he moved his hands about. "You don't have to have marzipan creams to live, do you? Or pineapple rings? Or a dab of scent? Well, there's some as do. Get what I mean? It's the greedy ones, with the cash to spare—they're what we're after. It'd be different if it was bread and veg we was marketing, but it's the trimmings these people want, and Freddy Straker's got 'em. And if you make 'em wait a bit, those fat bookies' wives, if you let 'em sag a bit first inside their corsets, you never have any problems getting a good price for your stuff. Take it from me—I know."

"Black market goods," Oxley repeated slowly. "That's what they are, and you want to use this house for them. That's correct, isn't it?"

"Safe as the Horse Guards, this place, and a guaranteed gold mine. And easy. You wouldn't have to give up anything you was doing already, you see. You could fit it in with your other line of business."

"Where does all this stuff come from?"

"Here and there." Freddy Straker moved his legs and settled himself squeakily back into the chair. "Special imported, I call it. Of course, some of it's pinched. Most of it's fiddled. I don't ask no questions. How else would you get it these days?"

"Where is it now? I mean, you do have the stuff, don't you? Or are these plans for the future? You're not just showing off?"

Freddy looked offended. "You think I'm just a loud mouth or something? There's a lorry loaded and waiting at my sister's out in Gidea Park right this minute. And

56

her tool shed's full up, too. As soon as I can get it into London, it's worth something—see? It's dead merchandise out there. I've got plenty of clients waiting here, and all of them breathing hard." Freddy leaned forward. "What's your line, anyway? I can see you've got a sound enough noddle."

Oxley held himself away from the light. "What do you think it is?"

"My God, you're an artful one, and no mistake. You don't give much away, do you? Never volunteer for nothing." Freddy sucked in his dark-red cheeks. "I was watching you reading those cards round by the station and down here on Cluster Street. You're in the get-together business, ain't you? Hanky-panky. Lonely Hearts. Slap and tickle. That's my guess. Not my speed, but you can't really go wrong with it, can you? War, slump, holidays—it's always good, no matter what." His voice was cocky. "I keep my eyes open. That's the way to get on." He waited. "That's it, isn't it?"

"All right, you can bring the lorry after dark tomorrow. There'll be space upstairs. I'll see to that tonight." Oxley terminated the interview.

"If you say so." Freddy's voice was quieter. "I'm not prying; but nothing underhanded, mind you, or we'll both cop it. I guarantee half and half, fair shares, like I said. Your line's your own affair, if that's how you want it."

"Tomorrow night. At about eight," Oxley said. He stood over Freddy Straker.

"We'll be doing all right in next to no time, mark my words."

"Yes," Oxley said slowly, "I'm sure of it. If they want it that badly, they'll have to make it worth somebody's while, won't they? One or two at a time, to begin with. Just a few for the beginning. Upstairs. And then, maybe, we can expand. They can come and beg for it, can't they? Make us feel sorry for them upstairs."

"Well, I dunno about only one or two. I was thinking of more than that—quick in, quick out. You know, big turnover, big and easy—that's what I really had in mind."

Oxley picked up the lantern by its wire handle and opened the folding doors. "Tomorrow evening around eight o'clock with the lorry, Straker. Push off now."

When he had bolted the door behind Freddy, Oxley extinguished the flame and left the lantern in the hallway. He felt his way through the black house into the room next to the front parlor, connected to it by the folding doors. He groped his way to his narrow pallet and sat there with his hands pulling at his face. Later he went out to eat; afterward he walked through the blackout for several hours where the crowds were thickest.

Eight

The late-afternoon chill from the street outside caught him just below the shoulder blades. He shivered and gripped tighter upon the handle of the machine. In perhaps another half-hour they would have to close the door—an open space in the planked-up front of the Amusement Arcade—and pull the blackout curtain over it to keep the electric light sealed in. It was disconcerting to look up from the little jerky toy in its glass case with finger marks everywhere and "Super Crane" written at the top, to see people on the pavement outside moving past the doorway. One of them before long was going to come in to find him, and then everything would begin.

At the back of the Amusement Arcade the owner coughed, a huge cough that set all the fat on his body shaking and made him hold onto his belly. But the cough went unheard. It was just a movement that Oxley observed among the clockwork noises, the ring of metal striking rusty metal, the dry rattle of machine parts that hadn't been serviced since the war began.

The owner turned his head to one side and spat. A shiny ball of phlegm rose from his mouth and fell somewhere inside the darkened rink where the Dodgem cars lay covered in tarpaulin for the duration. "Be Like Dad, Keep Mum," the poster behind him said.

The Super Crane stuck. Half-buried in green sugar beans, the jaws suddenly stopped. In the chromium base the mechanism whirred on.

A young boy with one knee bandaged and a large scab showing on the other stood next to him, rubbing his nose with slow intensity and watching him with screwed-up eyes.

"Lousy swindle." The boy wiped his nose with the sleeve of his jersey. "Give it a wallop." He looked over his shoulder to the owner at the back of the Arcade. "Want me to give it one for you, mister?" he said. He kicked at the base as he asked the question.

The crane did not move; down at the bottom the motor ran on with its pennyworth of time.

The owner sat reading the afternoon papers at a card table that faced the machines. Oxley saw him suck greedily on one of his thumbs and move it around in his mouth. By his elbow there was a gallon saucepan filled to the brim with pennies, and a pile of dog-eared cards that said: "Not Working Today. Try Me Another Time." His dentures soaked inside a glass of cloudy water behind the saucepan.

Oxley turned the machine handle all the way over, the boy kicked at the square base, and jaws started to move again.

The rolled-up copy of *Picture Post* under Oxley's arm was getting in the way.

"See, mister, what did I tell you?"

Oxley adjusted the magazine, rolled it tighter, pressed it harder under his armpit. He did not acknowledge the presence of the boy beside him.

"See?" The boy stepped back from the machine to admire his work. Then he came back to the Super Crane and stood side by side with Oxley. "What did I tell you? Now it's going, mister, why don't you try for the lighter?"

The steel jaws were smooth, so slippery they would hold nothing but a few sugar beans. A lighter probably made in Japan ten years before, and four tin cigarette

60

cases, some fancy key rings, playing cards done up in wads of blue paper like cotton wool, a small china spaniel—they looked as though they had been there since the day the machine was installed. They were impossible to budge; things were fixed that way. A few of the beans at the back near the electric light bulb had started to run, and there was green slime on the glass. The other machines at least rewarded customers with a big score marked up in colored lights, and it stayed there until the next penny went down the rusting slot. People had to have something for the time they spent, the concentration: sugar beans, a tin of fruit cocktail, a bottle of Tête-à-Tête.

The boy's cheek was pressed to the glass. He stared at the moving crane and tapped gently and rhythmically at the base of the machine with the toe of one boot.

"The other way," he said, "the other way. Go for the lighter: it's the best thing there. You can do it the other way. Try for the hump on it, mister—the hump. No!" He kicked wildly at the base. "The other way! Go on!" he said urgently, putting his hands all over the glass.

Oxley turned the handle. While he waited for the stranger, he probed after cheap goods he didn't want, ending up each time with a thimbleful of green beans gone runny. He thought of the woman from Maida Vale, Mrs. Lintott. She said she needed to have something put by in case of an emergency, like her old man on leave. She had been waiting nearly three months for the anchovies, with the money laid out in advance. Any day now, the new consignment—that's what he and Freddy told her—what can you expect in times like these? . . . Mrs. Lintott was one of the eager ones who came early, the minute the blackout was down. She wanted the anchovies, but it was clear that the game, the suspense, meant most to her.

The boy took his face away from the greasy glass.

"You going to keep trying? Have another bash at the lighter, mister."

Oxley looked carefully around the Amusement Arcade. He paid no attention to the boy.

The owner got up from the card table and walked down the Arcade toward the doorway, wiping his fingers on his apron. His mouth was full of shining teeth.

A soldier, forage cap perched at the back of his head, stopped him and said, "This one don't work. It ain't worth a light. I lost tuppence on the bleeding thing already."

The owner pointed to another machine over his shoulder. It was called "Let's All Go Down the Strand." "Try it," he said, fetching up a penny from his apron pocket, "and I'll give you another one of these when I've been and done the door." His speech was thick; the teeth seemed to be getting in his way. Farther down the Arcade he saw someone he knew. "Don't break the springs, Charlie," he said to a thin, worried-looking man on the platform of the Fate and Weight machine.

Oxley watched the owner pull the khaki curtain across the doorway. He had meant to wait over a cup of tea in the café next door and then come in here just before the appointed time, but when he got inside the café he saw that it was all mirrors from top to bottom, wall after wall, repeating images endlessly: a bright red scarf, cups, cutlery, people hunched over table tops, two young girls coming very slowly through the lavatory door—and he left quickly.

"Go on!" The boy was kicking at the chromium base. "Go on, go on!" He grabbed hold of Oxley's hand and tried to pull it away from the machine to make room for his own. But all he did was push Oxley's darkened skin harder against the red rubber.

62

Oxley snatched his hand away. He stepped back from the machine and the boy and almost tripped over. The owner was standing behind them. The boy had already let go of the handle.

"Come on, blast you," the owner said. He took a handful of jersey at the boy's shoulder with his huge, chapped hand. His gold wedding ring looked absurdly slim and tight, like wire around cheese. "Come on," he said. He started to drag the boy away.

"I'm with him." The boy caught hold of the handle. "I'm with him. Ain't I, mister? Tell him. Ain't I with you?"

"None of your bloody lip," the owner said.

"He's with me. Leave him alone. You heard what he said—he's with me." Oxley put another penny into the Super Crane's slot.

The owner went away. Oxley watched him drop his mouthful of teeth into the cloudy water and settle down with his papers again.

"Try for the hump, mister."

Halfway down the Arcade there was a man with gray hair and black ragged brows standing alone under a sign that said, Spicy Snapshots from Gay Paree. He was neatly dressed in a well-cut dark business suit. There were white points of handkerchief showing at his breast pocket, and a gold-mounted signet ring on his little finger. Flanked on either side by vending machines for chocolate, toffee, cigarettes—all empty, some with the glass smashed in—he looked abandoned, like well-made luggage among the litter of a station platform. Very slowly he turned the handle of What the Butler Saw. But he was not looking into the eyepiece for the jerky roll of photographs. Oxley saw that the man was looking over in his direction, was staring at the rolled-up copy of *Pic-*

ture Post under the arm of someone he did not yet know who stood with a boy at the Super Crane.

"Your time's not up yet, mister. Go on, have it out." The boy put a couple of green beans into his mouth.

"You can have it," he said. He turned his back to the boy. "Finish it up."

The man walked toward the Super Crane. In one of his socks there was a small pink hole. The man came up to them. He cleared his throat.

"Mr. Oxley?"

"That's right."

"Pleased to meet you. My name's Timpson." His mouth seemed dry. "Not too warm tonight, is it?" he said hesitantly.

"Live far?" Timpson said as soon as they were at the doorway of the Arcade.

Oxley pulled the khaki curtain back into place behind them: and then it was easy because they were in the blackout, the movement of Cluster Street after dark, the old smells.

Oxley gripped Timpson's arm and steered him toward the north. "You'll like it."

"Don't know this part one bit," Timpson said. "Not far, is it?" Then he stopped.

The canopy of a perambulator grazed against Oxley's hand. "What's up?" he said to Timpson, feeling the man wriggle from his grip.

Timpson drew a pencil torch out of his trouser pocket. He flashed the tiny weak beam to his feet.

Oxley caught roughly at his arm. "You don't need that thing. Put it out."

The torch smacked down upon the pavement and rolled into the gutter. It was still lit.

Someone bumped into them. People went by on their way to the pubs. "Strike me pink!" a man said. "Did you see that?" Someone else belched loudly and said, "Beg your pardon."

"Signaling to Jerry—see that?"

A young woman swore into the darkness, "You bastard!"

A man addressed the people bumping together on the black pavement, "See that?"

"See that, Alice?" another voice said.

Timpson clutched Oxley's sleeve. A woman breathed beer over them.

"See it? Of course I did! Do you think I'm blinded or something? What's the bastard up to, waving that thing around like his you-know-what? Keep the bloody thing down where it belongs!"

People were trying to get past on the pavement.

"See him waving it up to heaven like that?" another person said.

"It's one of them sly Irish buggers. Hanging's too good for that lot."

Inside the pram a child started to cry, and an old man shouted, "Shove the dummy in her mouth, for Christ sake!"

"Lilly," one of the women said, "Lilly, got it, Lilly?"

Someone bent down next to them, and a pair of high heels grazed against Oxley's ankles. He stepped behind Timpson and felt Timpson stumble as he tried to get out of the way.

"Yes, Vi, I have," another woman said. "It'll be nice for our Wilfy to have, won't it?"

"That's who I was thinking of."

Someone's arm nudged gently into them.

"Serves the bugger right to lose it, don't it, mate?"

Oxley pushed his way out of the group with his hand tight on Timpson's sleeve.

"Yids again," a man said behind them.

They walked on in silence, Timpson a little behind,

Oxley in front, drawing him through the blackout, past the muffled pub doorways, the bumping groups of people on their way to the pictures and the local hop, toward Jubilee Square and a cup of tea with Mrs. Lintott, waiting for them in the big room upstairs.

When the road opened out to the Square, Oxley felt a cold breeze cross his face. The road was deserted. They passed no one.

Timpson spoke: "I'm sorry," he said, "is it far now?"

"You'll like it," Oxley said.

Timpson cleared his throat several times. "It's a fine night," he said at last. "Quite a nip in the air, though." He stumbled on a piece of rubble.

Oxley stopped. "You ought to get used to moving around without a torch."

Timpson made an effort to loosen Oxley's grip upon his sleeve. Oxley felt the man's sweat across his crisp knuckles. "If you don't mind, I'll just get out my wallet—" Timpson said.

Oxley pushed him on. "Another time—later. We make no promises."

Inside the dead-silent hallway, as soon as Oxley had let go of his sleeve, Timpson said in a congested voice, as if he had been bottling up the words all day, "I'm not just after a bit of fun. It's friendship. The other's easy enough to find—only, you're as bad off afterwards as before. There's nothing to show for it, is there? I wouldn't be here now if it was just that."

Oxley said, "We make no promises. We'll have to see how things work out."

Everything in the room was red from the lamps—one on the floor under a tall felt panel where the window had been, the other on a shelf to one side of the cupboard. In

66

the crack at the bottom of the cupboard door there were small flakes of glass. When people crossed the room the glass flashed bright red sparks at their eyes.

Oxley stood by the woman and, while still looking at Timpson, pointed first at her and then over to Freddy Straker.

"This is Val Timpson—Mrs. Lintott. Freddy Straker —Val Timpson." He spoke slowly and distinctly.

Mrs. Lintott's hair was ginger-red, and the space between her two front teeth was a black line.

She looked up from her chair and smiled at Oxley, then at Freddy, then at Timpson. She wore a gray dress, heavy and tweedy, but with a very low V-neck that showed a pink triangle of her underwear. She addressed the newcomer: "I can never remember names right off. What was that again?" She leaned her head forward, shaking a fine stream of powder to the floor.

"Timpson. Val Timpson." He sat on the wide divan with his hands on his kneecaps. He blinked a couple of times. "No," he said, "I'm like you. Most of the time *I* can't either."

"You get used to the light after a while," she said. "Then you find it restful. Have you come far?"

"Belsize Park." He looked behind him. "Almost straight through. Only one change." The divan was too wide. In order to lean back he would have to take his feet off the floor and stretch his legs out.

Oxley watched him and the woman. The end of her full nose was flat, as if permanently pressed against glass.

Freddy called out, "Coming nicely to the boil." He bent over a little kerosene stove they had put inside the cracked and pitted fireplace. On the otherwise bare mantelpiece there was a white box and three cups and saucers.

A patent-leather handbag large enough to hold five pounds of potatoes leaned against the back of Mrs. Lintott's chair. It was the only chair in the room. Freddy had brought it up earlier in the day from the room downstairs.

"Do you have a cigarette?" she said to Timpson.

"No, I'm sorry. I don't smoke. If I'd known, though, I'd have tried to get some."

Oxley, rigid and still, stood back against the wall.

He said, "Mrs. Lintott, you're going to have to wait a bit longer for your anchovies. Val here's not in that line."

Timpson blinked. He cleared his throat. "Anchovies?"

She pulled the antimacassar from beneath her head and began to pluck at the red fringe. "Not put off again, am I?" she said. "And me with nothing in the larder in case of emergency. God only knows what we'll be reduced to by the time we're through with all this lot."

Freddy rattled the teapot lid. "Best cuppa this side of China."

"Freddy," Oxley said from his place by the cupboard door, "how's your time? I can finish all that."

Freddy put milk into the three cups, and then stood up. "Yes," he said, "I best push off, I expect." He turned to the woman. "Mrs. L"—he winked at her—"Mrs. L, your courage, your cheerfulness, your resolution, will bring us victory. No doubt in my mind about that, no doubt at all." He spoke in a sing-song voice and pointed around the room. "*Your* courage, *his* nerve, *my* noddle, and those blinking anchovies will be in your hands before you know it." He addressed each one in turn: "Mrs. L, Val, all, see you shortly. Cheerio."

No one spoke until they heard the front door slam downstairs.

"Good heart, that boy," Mrs. Lintott said.

Oxley handed them both a cup of tea.

A lorry backfired outside, and a few seconds later the noise of a motor came through the felted windows.

"Yes," Oxley said. "You need a good heart in times like these, don't you?"

The room was silent.

"Warm enough for you two in here?" Oxley asked.

"Lovely," she said.

"Quite chilly outside, though," Timpson said.

They sipped at the tea.

Oxley spoke to them: "Mrs. Lintott, Val brought a chocolate cake for you." He took a box of Balkan Sobranie cigarettes from his pocket and put them into Timpson's lap. "You forgot these," he said, turning to the mantelpiece and the white cake box.

Showing the space between her front teeth, she addressed Oxley: "You do have nice friends, I must say."

Timpson, on the edge of the wide divan, stretched an arm carefully down to the floor in order to rest his cup of tea by the side of his feet. He saw the hole in his sock and pulled his trouser leg down in a vain effort to cover it up. He fiddled with the cigarettes and offered her one. He had opened the packet at the wrong end.

Oxley put matches into his lap and then, on top of the matches and the packet of Balkan Sobranie, the white box.

Mrs. Lintott lifted the cigarette to her lips.

Timpson held the cake box with one hand and with the other reached, carefully and awkwardly, under it, into his lap, for the matches. Then, keeping the box steady between his elbows, he lit her cigarette.

"Watch out you don't crush it," she said after she had inhaled. Leaning forward in her slippery chair, she reached toward Timpson's lap. She shoved a pair of fin-

69

gers down the side of the box and pried up the lid. She saw the rich, uneven surface of the chocolate cake.

"Oh," she said, settling back on the chair, "that's a sight for sore eyes these days, isn't it?"

Oxley put his untasted cup of tea on the shelf by the roadman's lantern. Above the cake the white lid was flat and square against Timpson's chest.

"It makes all the difference to a pot of tea, doesn't it?" she said.

Timpson sat looking down at the cake. There was a finger mark on one side. "Yes, it does." He moved his feet, rattling the half-full teacup as he did so. Tea splashed into the saucer. He weighed the cake in his hands and looked up, as though for assistance, to where Oxley stood rigid and silent with his palms pressed flat against the wallpaper. But the glass at the cupboard door seemed to flash at Timpson's eyes. He put his hand up as if shading them, and after blinking nervously several times he looked down at the cake again.

Mrs. Lintott squashed out her cigarette in her saucer. "Feeling all right?" she said.

He looked helplessly at the cake upon his knees. "We need something to cut it with."

"What a life, eh?" she said, looking at the cake intently. "Do you really think Churchill's doing everything he could? I mean, everything? And why on earth the Yanks don't come in, beats me." She stared at the cake. "What a pretty ring," she said. "What sort of business are you in?" She smiled encouragingly.

His eyebrows joined momentarily. He looked toward Oxley and said, "Insurance."

"That's a good one these days." She giggled softly into her cup, then finished the rest of the tea. "Well," he said, "you take a chance with everything these days." He put

70

the cake box onto the divan next to him and took the cigarettes out of his lap.

"If it wasn't for people," she said, "I really wonder how we'd get through it all. I don't think you can stay on your ownsome all the time, do you? It's enough to drive you up the pole. It's different if you've got kids."

Timpson brushed his lap with small gestures. "No," he said, "that's what's wrong. People need company. A bit of harmless fun. To relax you. Take your mind off things." He spoke very fast.

"Yes," she said, "that's right. What I've always said is live and let live."

"A nice dinner and the Palladium afterward. Do you like Tommy Trinder? That sort of evening out makes all the difference."

"My word"—she moved her chair closer to him and the divan—"you *are* a tonic to talk to."

"Oh, no," he said quickly, "not at all," but he smiled at her and put out his hand, the one with the signet ring on it, to touch her, and for the first time that evening he showed his large, uneven teeth.

Oxley moved from the wall into the red glare. He looked down at them with his skin creased tightly at the mouth and at the eyes. He spoke through the fixed smile. "That's right. What did I tell you, Mrs. Lintott?"

Timpson held the woman's hand protectively. When he looked up at Oxley he blinked at the light and squeezed the woman's hand.

Oxley watched them. After a moment he spoke: "I have to go downstairs."

"Oh, yes," Mrs. Lintott said.

"Don't let me disturb your chat."

He went out of the door without looking back at Timpson and the woman leaning toward each other, or the dark stains left by his palms on the wall.

Downstairs, in the room with the folding doors, he sat by the dank clumps of ferns and plants. The house was completely silent, heavy and airless and still. He felt his heart stir with excitement as he waited. After a while he heard the floorboards above his head creak and resist the careful footfalls, the sound of the chair scraping, the divan being pushed hard against the wall.

Nine

The memory of what had happened in the big room upstairs found its way into everything Oxley did during the days that followed. In the mornings, behind the folding doors downstairs, when the tin alarm clock went off, the room's details—the creased cover of the wide divan, the mark of a shoe on the wall—settled upon his mind. They were with him at the Cluster Empire as people shifted their bodies in the warm air that carried always a faint, sharp smell of disinfectant; with him in the cafeteria while he ate; with him outside the shops where he read the postcards: the man (Box 23/PTOF/E.C.4) in need of discipline; the young married couple wishing to meet another ditto, view to friendship, any weekend May/July inclusive; the girl with one leg, interested in rubber clothes and physical photography. And the details were with him in the Amusement Arcade when, turning the worn handle of the Super Crane, he waited for the strangers, the men who wrote letters of assignation, the message placers from Bayswater and Chigwell and Tooting Bec. From the time he had stealthily moved after Timpson and the woman, silent up the stairs like smoke, to stand, waiting, watching, outside the blast-warped door, the details were fixed inside him—a foot thrashing; the unyielding, slippery chair with its burden of flesh; the moans. And, again, later in the night, after the couples had left, the signs of abandonment—the dirty mark on the wall, the smeared leather.

One afternoon as he was coming back across the Square from the cafeteria a postman stopped him.

"Here, mister, you live in the house, do you?"

"What house?" he said. All his letters came to a box number, and when he wrote he supplied no information except the meeting place, the date, the hour.

"That thing over there. No letterbox, no room under the door, no knocker. Man at the sweet shop says some-one lives here."

"Who's the letter for?" Oxley said.

"Name of Oxley at Number Five Jubilee."

"What's the postmark?"

The man looked up cagily. "That's for the bloke who gets it. Letters are private. You know the bloke, do you?"

"My name's Oxley."

But the man clearly did not believe him. "I'll walk you across," he said, and it wasn't until he saw Oxley insert the key and turn the lock that he handed over the letter. "I have to be careful. Good day."

The first thing Oxley looked at was the postmark. It said Salisbury. He felt afraid. Despite his precautions, he was being crowded out of his careful solitude, tracked down, found out.

But it wasn't his mother's writing. The hand was deliberate and overcareful, the hand of an infrequent pen-man. He tore the envelope open on the front step.

"Dear Mr. Oxley." He read the signature—"Mrs. G. Clatley," it said—and then he started from the begin-ning:

The rent money's coming through alright, it's not that. I would not trouble except for telling you your Mother has her knife into me and Ray Ray and we have moved Ray Ray and me to c/o Mrs. Hinchliffe,

74

42 Glenda Road, I suppose you know where it is. Your Mother does not know where you are, in my house. I hope you are looking after my things. Ray Ray is well and we hope the same of you. Your Mother is well, its doing her the world of good. She has an idea I know but I say nothing so she has her knife into me and Ray Ray. Your better off. Very truly,

and then the signature.

He went inside, into the lamplight, before the past could take hold.

After a while Mrs. Lintott started to bring a friend, a young woman from Sunderland whom she had mentioned several times. The woman had traveled south to keep her husband company when he finished his nightly shift on the guns in Hyde Park—only to find, when the long move was already made, that he had been sent west, without any warning, to Portland Bill. Refusing to budge from London, she had found work as a secretary and now wanted some silk underwear for the spring. Freddy made her laugh a lot and say chidingly, "You Londoners," in her harsh northern voice. They let her have some expensive lipstick and a pair of black patent-leather shoes to match her gas mask case. She got on well with Timpson, who came to the house now almost every night. And one evening Oxley brought back from the Amusement Arcade a captain in the Home Guard, a widower from Putney, his skin as smooth as blancmange, who told the women about Afghanistan while he prodded at the pimples behind his ears.

With his mackintosh belted around him, and a copy of *Picture Post* in his pocket, Oxley waited for the women in the dark front room. He opened the door before they finished knocking.

The sky behind them flickered with searchlights.

The women peered in upon him.

"By gum," the northern voice said, "you *are* sharp tonight."

The sky went black for a moment, and the stars shone. The night was cold and clear. Then the searchlights began to move across the sky again.

"Mrs. Fredge. Nice to see you, Mrs. Fredge. And Mrs. Lintott. Go straight up. Freddy's there, keeping Val and the captain happy. I'll be back shortly. I've got to meet a friend."

"And I," Mrs. Fredge said, "have got to see a man about a dog."

"Well, you know the way," Oxley said. "Freddy's put a light in there now. On the left of the basin."

They came in giggling and groped their way upstairs as he went out of the house.

"Oh, Dottie," he heard Mrs. Lintott say with a laugh just before he closed the door behind him, "you've got no shame."

He led the man to the top of the stairs, holding him tightly by the arm. They stood and watched through the crack of the badly fitting door.

Inside the big room they were all drinking: Mrs. Lintott and Val Timpson seated at the far edge of the divan, and, at the end nearest the door, the captain and Mrs. Fredge, before whom Freddy Straker stood holding up a roll of toilet paper. Freddy had unwound nearly a foot of it, and he waved the end, streamer-fashion, back and forth in the air. The paper was pale orange, then pink as it caught the light.

"Look at that," Freddy said, "just look at it." He lowered it a little closer to Mrs. Fredge's face. "Feel of it. Go on, don't be bashful, have a real good feel. Almost melts in your hands, don't it? It's enough to give you goose pimples." He stroked the paper gently with the tips of his fingers. "We won't get no more like that for the duration."

"It *is* nice," Mrs. Fredge said.

"I know women: you can't resist anything as lovely as that, can you?" He rewound the roll of paper. "Of course, it's a luxury item, not cheap at all—that goes without saying. Just one consignment of eleven rolls."

The captain kept a hand busy behind his ear. The other hand held a glass of stout and was pressed against the small of Mrs. Fredge's back.

"How much are you asking for it?" she said to Freddy, while looking all the time at the captain.

"We can't break up the consignment, of course, but— I'll tell you what"—Freddy tore off three orange pieces with great care not to leave the roll too ragged at the end—"take a piece home with you, and *then* see."

"Yes, but how much?"

"Try it first," he said.

"The undies." She sipped her Bass. "I'd love to have them in the same sort of apricot color." She turned her body around to face the captain. "Isn't it a pretty shade?"

"Don't worry yourself about those undies," Freddy said. "As soon as I can locate the right gent you'll get them. Haven't let you down yet, have we?" Freddy nudged the captain. "Tell her how lucky she is not to be called up. She'd be wearing nothing but woolen passion killers for the duration."

The other couple looked up at Freddy and laughed. The captain drank down the rest of his beer. Mrs.

77

Fredge smiled for a moment into her empty glass and then put it on the leather seat of the single chair.

Then Oxley and the new man walked in. The others all shifted a little and smiled.

The room, except for the floor, was almost completely unchanged: the felted windows were the same, and the glass inside the cupboard, the bare mantelpiece, the cracked walls. But the floor was clothed and soft now. There was a prewar figured carpet made to order for a Turkish bath in Bristol that had never opened. It was too large for the room, and on one side it was rolled under for nearly three feet. Thrown down carelessly upon it were a few cushions. In a holder by the fireplace there were new light bulbs, not yet switched on, white and unshaded.

"This is Mr. Rains." Oxley let go of the man's arm.

They all looked at the stranger, at his narrow, youthful face, his pinched eyes. The top lid of one of them was fat and inflamed. He held out a hand to Mrs. Fredge.

Oxley called over to Mrs. Lintott: "Mrs. L, you're still interested in those anchovies, aren't you? Because if you are, you ought to be especially nice to Mr. Rains."

Mrs. Lintott moved toward the edge of the divan. "Oh, I should say I am! Any friend of those anchovies is an automatic friend of mine."

Timpson shifted himself closer to her.

Oxley took the empty glass off the leather seat of the chair. "Take a pew, Mr. Rains." He turned to Freddy and nodded. "Mrs. Fredge," he went on, "you look as though you're ready for a refill. Mrs. L, another little drop of wallop for you? Mr. Rains, you'll have a glass of Bass?"

The two couples leaned together on the wide divan, faced by Rains, slippery on the single chair.

Freddy waved good-bye. "I'm off after those undies, Mrs. Fredge."

She waved back and then drained her glass in one go.

"Have no fear," Freddy called from the door. "And let me know about that paper when you finish with the sample. Toodle-oo, all."

Oxley topped all the glasses with beer. Mrs. Lintott spoke animatedly to Rains. She smiled, drank, told him how rude the salesgirls were getting in the big shops, especially Larson's. Rains, quiet and flushed, leaned forward in his chair. His mouth worked as though he were chewing. Timpson and the captain sat with Mrs. Fredge between them and spoke about the war. Timpson was telling her of a near-escape he had overheard at the office. The captain, his hand still at his ear, changed the subject to malarial fever, then to Gandhi, then to the behavior of Canadian soldiers on leave in London. He began to raise his voice. Mrs. Fredge turned from one to the other encouragingly. Their glasses moved, sparkled pink and brown in the light, their lips glistened, their voices grew louder.

Rains splashed beer on Mrs. Lintott's skirt. He leaned over to wipe it off. Swift as a hawk she bent toward him.

"What a nasty sty. Looking through too many key-holes, eh?"

The captain took his hand from his ear and began to play with the buttons at the back of Mrs. Fredge's dress.

"I don't have to look through keyholes. I leave that sort of thing to those who need it."

"Your eye looks fierce. Rub it with gold." Mrs. Lintott tried to turn her wedding ring. "Put your head down. A couple of gentle strokes should do the trick all right. Here"—she addressed Timpson, drew him into the circle—"give us a hand. It won't come off without a real good tugging."

She drank down the rest of her beer while Timpson pulled at the ring.

"Go on," she said to Rains, "put your head down like a good boy."

Mrs. Fredge was singing "Bless Them All." The captain beat time on her knee with the bottom of his glass. Rains squeezed himself onto the divan next to Mrs. Lintott, and Timpson laid his hand on the side of her neck. Shivering and giggling, she reached up to take hold of the hand, then touched her glass on Rains's cheek. When his thigh moved toward her flesh she fell back on the divan, laughing and squealing and dripping her fresh glass of Bass. Mrs. Fredge started up with "All the Nice Girls Love a Sailor." Rains reached to the floor for a cushion and put it behind Mrs. Lintott's head. The moment she was nestled against it she joined raucously in the singing. Rains began snapping his fingers in rhythm with the tune; it was like the sound of balloons breaking. His face came suddenly alive, and he put his mouth over Mrs. Lintott's. Mrs. Fredge fell back with the captain and Timpson, Timpson holding her by the waist from inside her unbuttoned dress, his other hand at Mrs. Lintott's breast under the thin-fleshed weight of Rains. Mrs. Fredge's voice sank into the captain's breath. Mrs. Lintott, with her legs in the air, tried to pull her shiny, wrinkled skirt down over the tops of her stockings. She was wearing garters made of white sateen. She hiccuped as she flailed the air with her foot. She sent the glass flying off the divan, hiccuped again, thrust one hand inside Rains's jacket, gave a tight hard moan, grazed her nails against Timpson's pink calf, moaned again, hiccuped, moaned, and then, quite suddenly, was still. Still and silent, with the moaning caught like a fish bone in the back of her throat.

The sirens were blowing.

Mrs. Fredge lifted her head. "Jesus Christ All-Bloody-Mighty," she said very quietly. Then she slumped back and lay without a movement, her flesh bared, her clothing crumpled, listening to the thin soughing that came through the felted windows from the streets outside.

The captain slid to the floor, trembling with small malarial spasms. Timpson's hands fiddled surreptitiously among his trouser buttons. Rains stood up, his lips clenched thin and tight.

Oxley opened the door.

"You could do with a bit more light in here, don't you think?"

He switched on the electric light bulbs. His guests turned their eyes from the brightness.

Rains sat down on a cushion. Mrs. Fredge tried to pull her dress together, tried at the same time to wipe the saliva from her face. Hiccuping once more, Mrs. Lintott blushed, put her arms over her breasts. There was a black and blue mark on one side of them. Timpson, on the edge of the divan, grasped his calves and stared at the shaking hand of the captain trying to hold a cigarette still.

The sirens stopped abruptly.

With his hands thrust deep into his pockets, Oxley walked to the middle of the floor. He looked down on them.

Airplane engines hummed somewhere in the high distance; they all raised their heads toward the sound. Nearby an antiaircraft gun began to fire.

His gaze encompassed them. When he spoke his voice was low and soothing:

"Nothing to be alarmed at. Just a little bit of excitement out on the coast. Don't look so upset, Mrs. Fredge, you're as safe as you can be here. This house has already caught a packet; it's not likely to get another one. Besides, they're not after people like us. Just carry on with the social as if nothing happened. We mustn't let the Jerries get us down, must we?"

And then he left them, the bright light shining in the silent room, and went downstairs to his narrow pallet.

After the All Clear had blown like a clean wind through the night, he listened to them leave the house. The water pipes rattled and washed through the walls a couple of times, the front door opened and closed. Everyone, even the women, left singly.

Ten

Just after he had returned to the house and was still feeling his way from the hall into the parlor, he heard someone knocking at the front door—sharply, insistently, without stopping. It sounded like a series of mallet blows. The knocking continued until the moment he opened the door.

A young girl stood in front of him holding a brown shoe. She looked down at it for a moment and said, "There isn't any knocker on the door." She was flushed and sounded out of breath. She wore a green scarf around her head. "I don't like disturbing you," she said, "but I saw you go in, and I thought you might know. I shouted at you from the other side of the Square, but you didn't hear me."

"What do you want?" He kept back inside the doorway.

"It's the gasman," she said. "They told me he lives up this way. Do you know where?"

The afternoon was full of scudding clouds. She raised her foot and, steadying herself against the doorjamb, slipped the shoe on again.

As she put her hand out he instinctively drew himself away from it. He noticed the paleness of her hair. He saw how slight she was beneath her thick woolen coat.

"No, I can't help you," he said. "Sorry."

He made a movement to close the door, but she started to speak again.

"I didn't mean to bother you. It's just that the meter's so full up we can't get another penny in it. My dad's been on all week about smashing it open, but you can't do that—even just to put more money in."

He saw how the wind sent the short ends of her hair scattering across her temples. He felt tired. From every part of the Square the light jumped before his eyes. She bit the inside of her bottom lip.

"Wouldn't you like to come in for a minute?" he said.

"Oh, that's very nice of you, but I really must find him straight off. My mum's trying to get Dad's supper ready; he's got to have something when he finishes work. I don't mind it for myself, but eating out every night's not the same for a grown man, is it?"

He stepped outside the door, which framed him in the shadow. He tried to smile at her across the daylight. When she saw his face she put the back of her hand, quite automatically, up to her cheek. As she moved, the tiny diamond on her finger caught the light.

He could see that she was young. Eighteen, perhaps, or nineteen. He looked at the slender, smooth wrists. He said, "I don't know anybody who lives round here. Have you tried telephoning the office?"

The light penetrated every pore in his skin. His face and hands felt bruised by the exposure.

"They *swore* he moved up here," she said. "The telephone box on our corner caught it in the Blitz, and, anyway, all they do is promise to come when they can. My dad'll be home in an hour and a half. If I could only find the gasman, I'd make him come with me." She doubled up her fist and pushed it into the pocket of her coat. "I'd like to see him refuse."

"I don't know anybody who lives around here. Why don't you come in, and I'll see what I can do about it."

"Do you have a telephone?"

"No, I'm afraid I don't." He thought how easy it would be to shut the door, to go back inside the house and leave her out there in the daylight. But without warning, her eyes filled up with tears. She turned her head away. He saw how slim her neck was. As the scarf slipped to one side he saw the pale tufts of down at the nape of her neck.

He held a hand out to her. "There's a portable stove upstairs. You can take it home for now and then call the gas office afterward. They'll probably send someone round tomorrow."

"Won't you be needing it yourself? I'm not going to deprive you—"

"Come inside the parlor, and I'll get it down for you. It's on the top floor."

When he reappeared she was crocheting a doily. He found her bent over toward the red glow, almost touching the lantern with her cheek. Her coat was still buttoned up and her scarf was pulled more securely over the top of her head. She wrapped the doily around the needle and put it into her pocket. She got up.

"The light, it can't be very good for your eyes," she said, trying to help him with the stove.

"You get used to it after a while," he said. "The stove's not heavy. You'll be able to manage it quite easily."

"Do you think it's going to work? I can see it hasn't been put to too much use lately. You use gas, do you?"

"I always eat out. We'll try and light the stove here first."

"All that artificial stuff they use in food these days, it's not good for you in the long run."

He put the stove on a chair and went into the adjoining room to fetch the bottle of oil he kept by his bed. He moved through the darkness as though he had never been used to anything else and the dim disordered pallet behind the folding doors was part of the only existence he had ever known. He could feel his skin relax, his eyes stop smarting as he went about in the dark.

When he came back she was looking at the aspidistras. "They're dry as tissue paper."

"Nothing you can do about it. They need the daylight. I watered them for a few weeks at the beginning, but that's not enough. Without proper light they just get like boiled cabbage." He closed the folding doors behind him.

"Were you here," she said, "when the big one, the mine, came down?"

He unscrewed the bottle and began pouring oil into the stove. "No, I was miles away. Miles and miles. Didn't even know about it. I was busy, you might say, with other things." His hands were greasy from the bottle. "It's a long time ago now, isn't it?" His voice was harsh. "Lots of changes." In the dimness of the room he felt himself safe enough to give way to bitterness for a moment.

She nodded. "Time really flies. We're lucky it does, I suppose. This lot'll be all over before you can say Jack Robinson. Then things will be easier."

"Will they?" He looked at his hands, shining and hairless.

"You've gone and got into a mess. Look at that grease. I *am* sorry. Don't get it on your suit." She took a page of carefully folded newspaper from one of her pockets and then crumpled it up.

"You seem prepared for any emergency."

"I really didn't mean to put you to all this bother." She started to wipe at his hands. "We heard it land. It made a terrible racket when it exploded, I can tell you.

We live up along the canal. We almost got drenched through in the shelter, and every one of the sandbags was ripped to shreds. We had to go and get all new ones, though we use the underground shelters now. They said there wasn't any casualties." She stopped wiping his hands as though she had thought of something important. "No one dead. But you can't ever really believe what they tell you. They don't want to scare people. I was quite young then. Used to think going to the shelter was fun."

"Yes, I know. Things hadn't really got going at that stage, had they? There was still a lot of fun in everything then."

"There still is," she said, "for some."

"Yes, I suppose there is."

He lit the stove. The flame caught him off guard. Hastily he turned the wick downward. He closed the little glass door, and it glowed the color of amber. "Some people are having the time of their lives," he said. "Never had it so good. There are some who'll be sorry when the war's over. They'll have to draw their horns in then."

"Oh, thank you," she said. "I was so worried about my dad's supper. It's not fair for him. It makes all the difference when people are helpful. I'll bring you some oil back with the stove tomorrow. Will that be all right—tomorrow—or do you need it sooner?"

"No, that's not necessary. Just bring it back whenever it's convenient." He turned the stove off.

"Look, we've got a little spirit lamp we never use. It would give you a bit of light, make it a bit more cheerful in here until you can get some glass put back in the windows."

"No, please don't bring the lamp. I don't have any need for it."

"But I've imposed on you so much. It really wouldn't be any trouble."

"I wouldn't use it. I don't have any need for things like that." He picked up the stove and walked out into the passageway.

"Well," she said, "I'd best be getting home. Mum will be ever so pleased. I finish work at three."

"Why don't you just keep it until you can get the gas working again? The day, though," he said carefully, looking at her face as he spoke, "is better than at night. We entertain a lot in the evenings. I'm entertaining some married people"—he corrected himself—"married friends tonight."

"Well, then, tomorrow, without fail. I'm going to call the Gas, Light and Coke Office as soon as I drop this at home."

In a minute she would be gone. He thought of her standing out in the Square, smiling and frowning in the light.

"Maybe you'd like to come round one evening. I have people in all the time. It's quite jolly and sociable."

"You're a real gentleman." She took hold of the stove. "But I hardly ever go out anywhere after supper any more. We're always off to the underground as soon as it gets dark. Besides"—she opened the front door, and the light spilled in all around her body—"I'm still in mourning. In a manner of speaking. But—all the same—thank you very much."

And then she was gone out into the afternoon, the grimy stove in her arms, the green scarf flapping at her neck, toward the ragged victory gardens and the houses on the other side of the canal.

Eleven

Oxley found himself thinking about her the next day. But only when the house was quiet and he was alone.

Early in the afternoon Freddy got ready to go to the West End. There was a new business acquaintance to see, a sergeant in the American Army. Freddy had been watching the Americans ever since the moment, a few weeks before, when they first appeared on the London streets. People used to smile indulgently at them then, what with the chewing gum, the funny hats, the number of medal ribbons and bars. But Freddy took them seriously right from the start. He made them feel at home, helped with directions and the proper price for a girl, tried to find out if they had any goods for sale. He met the sergeant, tipsy and lost, coming out of the underground lavatory in Piccadilly Circus. It was easy work for Freddy. Over a glass of beer in Ward's Irish Bar the first transaction was arranged: twenty-three fountain pens from the P.X.; then cigarettes if all went well, and watches. Freddy was to pick up the pens today. He was elated by the new contact. He wore his most expensive suit, with hand-stitched lapels and a long wide drape from the shoulders, and he took more than an hour to get himself ready.

The girl didn't cross Oxley's mind until Freddy had gone. Except for the wind shaking the felted windows every so often, the house was still. Upstairs, the big room

89

was empty. He had cleaned it himself. The cushions were plumped up again; the divan cover, though permanently wrinkled, was back in its proper place; the carpet had been wiped off with rags and hot water. It was ready for another hospitable evening. Freed from the thick odor left by the previous night's social, when the two married couples, embarrassed only at the beginning, finally relaxed, changed partners, lay in the same room calling and moaning across to one another—husband to wife, wife to husband—in their excitement.

He thought of the girl. It was a quarter to four. She hadn't kept her promise to return. Perhaps they were still using the stove. She had put her hand to her cheek as though his scars were catching. With his fingertips he traced the ridges that led from his neck to his mouth. He thought of her slight body and the black coat buttoned around it for mourning. But on her head there was the bright green scarf, as if to acknowledge that everything —grief, the sense of loss—was used up and discarded. He thought of what it would be like with the raids over, the soldiers back home, the streets lit up. All at once he wanted to get outside; he couldn't bear any longer to sit by his unmade bed in a borrowed house waiting for good times to return. He snatched the front door open and went into the afternoon.

He walked round to the back of the house, kicking savagely, over and over, at a piece of brick. The violence calmed him. The brick bounced through the weeds and fell splashing into the canal, where a bicycle tire floated. Refuse lay among the grass and weeds that straggled along the embankment—a gas mask gnawed and befouled by rats, empty cigarette packets bleached white, small puddles of food shimmering with bluebottles and tumblebugs.

Directly across the canal from him were the victory

gardens. Farther along, past the iron footbridge, a row of houses. Beyond, he saw factory chimneys pouring forth black smoke, County Council flats like ancient barracks, and above everything the motionless silver girth of a barrage balloon.

There was a woman in trousers collecting her washing. A woman shouting at her over the back gardens. A little boy throwing stones into the canal from the middle of the footbridge. A noisy wireless set. A man who emptied a pail of dark green slops onto the grass bank. And, hovering in the fading afternoon, the living smell of cooking.

Just after half-past five Freddy returned. He was proud of the pens, streamlined and exotically American, and he laid them out for Oxley's approval as lovingly as if he had manufactured them himself.

"Them Yanks," he said admiringly several times. "I don't hold with all that talk about them. They're streets ahead of us." From his wallet he took out a prophylactic kit, already opened. With great care he spread the contents on his palm one by one. "It's all here. Everything and more. You couldn't even catch a cold with all this lot on. And they *give* them away. Free. Everything they do makes us look old-fashioned. And see these." He pulled at one of the pens. The top came off with a plopping sound. The nib was inflexible as a nail, and he moved it about in the lamplight so that it gave off small red flashes. "They'll go like hot cakes. You can't beat the Yanks for luxury. Them buggers, they don't hardly know what to give their soldiers next. How they remember there's a war on beats me."

"The Betsies," Oxley said. "They'll go for the pens. You could sell one to Mrs. Betsie tonight. Tell her what a lovely surprise it would make for hubby." He remembered how she had jerked her head away from the other man's mouth and moaned across the floor to her husband, how she had kissed his neck afterward, fondled the black and blue mark the other woman had raised. "They seem really devoted to one another, don't they? Especially the wife, Mrs. Betsie—though, it's true, she was very nice to Mr. Widdop also. She's not selfish when it comes to her friendship."

"Oh, her," Freddy said, "She's all tits and eyebrows."

"Don't be like that, Freddy, she's just a sociable type." She had put her hand heavily into Widdop's lap long before her husband had even touched Mrs. Widdop. "She's just bighearted, that's all."

"Well, I'll make her wait a long time for something as lovely as one of these pens. I'll show her what they look like, mind you, but she won't get one. Not just yet, anyway. There's still that crate of anchovies upstairs. Or the sack of onions. Not that I like the idea of letting her have the onions, either, but the bloody things'll be sprouting like hollyhocks if we keep them much longer. And she can pay through the nose for them. Mrs. Widdop—now she's the one for a nice Yank pen. She keeps on about a tin or two of Golden syrup, but we'll let her have a pen instead. And maybe some notepaper to go with it. She can write to the other woman's husband, Mr. Betsie, when she feels like going over the fun they had together."

"Freddy," he said, "you're an expert. It's a good idea to keep them dangling, otherwise they take it for granted —then they won't appreciate how lucky they've been to run into us, will they?" The extra refinements pleased him. Not just the odd surreptitious liaisons of the beginning, like Mrs. Lintott, but the adultery together, under each other's eye, like a family game. And afterward, back together, they were very affectionate: they held

92

hands and kissed, as though with renewed interest in each other.

"I'm beginning to feel like a counselor for young married couples," Oxley said, "with a guaranteed solution for all their personal problems."

"That Mrs. Betsie's not so bloody young. I hate to hear a woman swear like that—effing and blinding the way she does. I never have liked it. I don't mind the rest of it one bit; if that's what they like to get up to, that's their business. When you need it, you need it. But swearing's something else. My old lady, she liked her pint, all right, but she never used bad language. I'd like to have wiped that Mrs. Betsie across the mouth with the back of my hand for the way she carried on last night. What she needs is a good rake-over by an expert."

"She was just excited, that's all. We can wear her down soon enough." He turned sharply. There was a knock at the door.

In a moment Freddy had shoveled up the pens and pushed them into his trouser pockets. "Who the hell's that now? If it's a bleeding warden again, I'll spit right in his eye."

"I'll go," Oxley said, "I know who it is." When he drew back the bolts his hands were wet.

The stove was tied up in brown paper and string. It was the first thing he saw, the bulky parcel smelling of oil and stewed carrots. She pushed it toward him as soon as he opened the door. She was out of breath again, and apologetic: "Have you been needing it? The gasman's only just emptied the meter."

In the twilight everything about her seemed pale. The hands around the parcel, the anxious face above, tied now in a yellow scarf, they looked almost phosphorescent. Only the coat was black and without light.

"Here, let me take it. You'll come in for a minute or two, won't you?"

Her skin was as smooth as oilcloth against his hand. They touched only for an instant, but at the contact he felt his stomach contract with fear.

"Only just emptied it," she said, following him. "I'm terribly sorry. Only just. Imagine the sauce of that. Otherwise I'd have brought it back earlier, like I said. Have you been waiting for it? I really am sorry."

"No, I told you, I never use it. You could have kept it for as long as you needed it."

He watched her closely. At first, in the red lamplight, she might have been one of the regular callers—except for the lack of calculation in her voice.

"My dad didn't half give him a piece of his mind, I can tell you. By the way, I didn't forget your oil." She took a half-pint milk bottle out of her pocket. Like the stove, it was wrapped in brown paper. "Oh, hello."

"Hello," Freddy said.

"This is a friend of mine. Freddy Straker—I don't know your name, I'm afraid."

"No, that's right, you don't. I mean, that's what was so nice about lending us the stove. I could have been anyone. It's Reever. Jessie Reever." She took Freddy's hand. "Pleased to meet you, I'm sure. This gentleman's been kind enough to lend us his oil stove. We had trouble with the gasman."

Her expression had hardly changed. Even when she spoke.

"And I can tell you, you'll keep on having it," Freddy said, looking away and speaking as though to no one in particular, "because they spend all their time getting off with the housewives."

Oxley saw that he did not even pretend to be interested in her. She was obviously the sort of girl he had known all his life. Good for a bit of fun after an evening at the pictures and a plate of fish and chips. Freddy patted the sides of his hair. He was less self-conscious playing up to people with more money in their pockets.

"Treating people like that!" she said. "They haven't got any consideration at all."

"Wouldn't you like to sit down?" Oxley said.

"Well, just for a moment, thanks. My mum, by the way, wanted me to thank you properly, she said, for lending us the stove. She says it was a blessing. I've been wondering all day what we could do in return. So I've brought you this. With our thanks."

She reached into her pocket. It was a little paper bag. "Go on, please take it. We appreciate your help."

He took the bag. He made no move to open it up.

"I hope you aren't going to feel offended." She smiled at him. Then she put the smile up quickly, as though she was uncertain about what she had done.

The bag was still closed in his hand. "Thank you. There wasn't any need—for anything, anything at all. You shouldn't have felt indebted. It was nothing."

"Well, neither's this, is it? I didn't mean to offend you."

He opened the bag. He pulled out two small bars of sweet milk chocolate.

Freddy laughed. "Jesus Christ Almighty. That's a real ripe one, I must say."

Oxley held the chocolate out toward her.

She flinched from the sound of Freddy's laughter behind her. "I didn't mean to offend anybody. But it's not that easy to get these days, and I thought you—"

"No, you're right, it isn't," Freddy said. "That's why we like to have so much of it handy around the house." He rattled the fountain pens aggressively in his bulging trouser pocket and strutted toward her.

Oxley was surprised at his own anger. "Freddy," he

95

said, "don't you have to get busy upstairs? Before all the guests arrive?"

"Oh, yes. Of course, mate. Of course I will. Happy to have met you, Miss." He was apologetic now, and respectful. "A very nice thought indeed." He waved at the chocolate.

She smiled again for a moment. Her cheeks shone in the lamplight, and her young eyes looked pale. They were paler than her hair.

Oxley clasped the chocolate as if it might fly out of his hand. "I don't know how to thank you."

"It's you who need the thanking. That stove, it saved our fat. My dad's got a bit of a temper, I don't mind telling you. But, of course, he works long hours nowadays, and there's all sorts of things on his mind—overtime and fire watching at the factory, as well as the rest. It'll melt, you know, holding it."

He did not know what to do with the chocolate. "Would you like some?" he said.

"Oh no, of course not. It's for *you*. That's what I brought it for. Naturally, give your friend—Mr. Whatsisname—a bit, if you want to."

He found himself waiting for her to smile again. During the few, separated moments in which she allowed her smile to appear, he saw that her eyes were like clear water.

"He works for you, does he?"

"Freddy Straker? What gives you the idea that Freddy works for me?"

"You can tell who's the governor here, can't you?"

Above their heads, he heard the sound of footfalls moving around, of Freddy Straker being occupied.

"Married friends of ours," Oxley said absently. He put the chocolate on the mantelpiece. It was like taking off handcuffs.

"Don't you ever go to the shelters at night, now that them rocket things have started coming over?"

"The raids don't bother me. The Jerries aren't really after people like me. I've more important things to do. They keep me busy."

"Well, I don't know who it is they're after, but it is safer down there. Besides, I like it in the Underground. Being with everyone helps to take your mind off things. You know everybody's in the same boat down there. It's very friendly. It doesn't do any harm to get out of yourself a bit, does it? You have to be sociable sometimes, otherwise you're done for. But, of course, if you have people in the house all the time, that's different."

She stared at him as she spoke. He kept waiting for her to take her eyes from his face. He walked into a shadowed corner of the room.

"Is your fiancé in the Army?"

"How did you—?" she began. She put both of her hands self-consciously into her coat pockets. "He *was.*"

"Is he discharged? Wounded?"

"He's gone," she said. "Last year in Libya." She stared into the corner where he stood shadowed and apart. "Time flies."

"Sometimes. It does, sometimes." And then: "I'm sorry."

"Time flies," she said again. "He was a good boy. Quiet in his ways but good as gold. You wouldn't think there was anything to him to begin with, till you knew him."

"You're a nice girl. You deserve better luck."

"There's always a lot to do."

"Is that the only way?"

"It's the best. It doesn't help to take on, though it's natural at first. There's his mum and dad and his brothers and sisters left also. There's more people involved in something like this than you think at the start. You're done for if you think you're the only one with any feelings. You have to get on with things the best way you can."

He sat down near her. There was nothing to say in face of her calmness.

"Especially now," she continued. "We all do. We'll get the war over with and see where we all are. Things'll be different then."

"Do you think they will?"

"Oh, of course—they've got to be. That's why we're in it, isn't it?"

"Yes," he said, "I suppose you're right. Things'll be different."

She went on: "I'm sure Mum would enjoy having you over for a cup of tea sometime. She told me to ask you, if I felt like it. For company's sake. Would you like to come?"

He saw her eyes fixed upon his face again. He forgot her calm mourning voice. His skin tautened with the sudden sarcasm of his words.

"Do you think I ought to go out more, get busy, make the time fly?"

She looked away, but his skin did not relax across his flesh.

"Oh, I didn't say that. We'd like to have you over to the house, that's all. Just for company."

All at once her sympathy leapt out clearly to him; it frightened him. She was sorry for him. She was trying to help, to be kind. Any minute she'd be telling him to use the shelter. Go to the pictures. Start taking girls out again.

But, instead, she stood up.

"Well, I really ought to be off to the Underground. I wish you'd come over sometime, I do. You've been such

98

a gentleman about the stove and all. It's not far. The Council tenements just off Stephen's Terrace. Nothing fancy, but it would be a real treat for us to have you in anytime you'd like to come. I mean it." Her eyes looked even paler now. She stood directly in the light of the lamp.

"Thank you," he said, and then added, "You're very kind."

It was as if he had been holding his breath without meaning to. He felt hot and dry, and his body burned. Not just his face—she had stared at it in the lamplight; even through the shadow in the corner of the room—but his entire body. Her sympathy had touched him like something alive. His skin itched. He wanted to tear at his body. He raised his hands to scratch his face, but he saw her watching him again and he dropped them quickly. He wiped his hands against the sides of his trousers. He thought of the hospital, coming to, feelings returning, and then pain. And afterward the fear, when he realized what the difference was. He felt vindictive as he looked at her.

"No," she was saying, "you're the one who's very kind. How about coming next Thursday?"

Her eyes rippled when she moved in the light; they looked as if she might have wept all the color out of them.

"Yes," he said slowly, "I'd like to. If you'll pay us a return visit here one evening."

"Oh, maybe I'll be able to do it. But is four o'clock all right for next Thursday? It's Eleven Tunstal Buildings across the canal. You can't miss it."

Twelve

There were three grimy blocks of flats in an asphalt yard; it was like an elementary school playground except for the iron posts that held washing lines. A pair of brick pillars marked the entrance to the yard; the railings and the gates had gone for war scrap. From behind the flats a brewery filled the air with the smell of hops and dray horses. Up on the wall of the flats, "Tunstal Buildings, Nos. 100-158," was spelled out in blue ceramic tiles.

Without going into the yard he walked around the flats looking for Number Eleven. He carried a square parcel.

He had not planned to bring anything with him. A little while before, on the other side of the canal, he had left Mrs. Clatley's house, had stepped into the Square with the daylight all around him, and had come to a sudden stop. In the bright leveled Square he felt completely exposed. He looked down at his hands, as if there were something they should be occupied with. He went back inside the house and stood in the darkness of the hallway, not knowing what to do. He touched his throat and stood feeling himself. He was afraid of leaving the house, knocking at a strange door. He would take her something. He thought of her pale eyes and of how her hair fell across her temples. He groped his way into his room. On the floor there was a pile of parachutes Freddy had bought from an Air Force sergeant. He reached down and took one from the middle of the pile. He thrust his hand deep inside the stiff canvas packing until his fingers reached the soft, warm silk; as he moved his fingers he felt his skin catch and grate against the delicate smooth interior. He put a piece of brown paper around the parachute and went out of the house. He held the parcel in both hands against his chest. He felt less afraid with something to hold, something to deliver.

He tried to make out the numbers of the flats he was passing. A couple of little girls swung a skipping rope for a boy in short trousers. The boy jumped up and down with his eyes shut tight. As they swung the rope the girls chanted: "One, Two, Three-a-Lairie; One, Two, Three-a-Lairie." The rope caught in the boy's legs. He opened his eyes as he fell to the ground, and then began to cry. As soon as he saw Oxley looking at him he stopped crying. He sat on the pavement with the skipping rope tangled around his legs and the two girls giggling above him, and stared in surprise at Oxley. The girls stopped giggling when they saw him. One of them pulled the pink slide out of her hair and put it in her mouth. Oxley hobbled away from them into the yard.

Number Eleven was on the ground floor next to the incinerator. Around the chute the asphalt was littered with dried-out tea leaves and bits of bread. The door of Number Eleven was a faded green color. As he touched the black knocker he heard the high voices of children running across the yard. He kept his eyes on the whitened stone step with its small piece of linoleum to tread upon.

He expected to see her when the door opened, but it was a middle-aged woman wearing a snood and a brown pinafore, a woman with thin lips and small features. Until she smiled he couldn't see the resemblance. Then, when she stopped smiling, she averted her gaze.

"You're Mr. Oxley, are you?" she said, staring at the

brown parcel. "Ever so pleased to meet you," and she stood to one side to let him into the passageway.

"Jessie, the man's here," she called out. He squeezed past her with the parcel held to his chest, and she pressed herself back against the open door, drew in her breath, and lifted her head high in the air. When she closed the door behind him the narrow passageway was suddenly dark.

He heard Jessie's voice somewhere in front. "You didn't have any trouble finding it, then?" she said.

His eyes finally adjusted to the dimness; he could tell that all the doors were open, as if to allow as much light as possible into the passageway. He looked for Jessie and saw, first, three small dark rooms and, then, a scullery full of steam, where Jessie stood over a boiling kettle.

"We're ever so glad you could come." Jessie moved toward him with a plate of sandwiches in her hand. "I hope you like sardine paste. It's prewar." She went ahead. "In here, in the parlor."

"Ever so pleased to meet you," Mrs. Reever said without moving. "Why don't you have a chair?" She stood by the table, looking down at the tea things until he was seated. "Jessie," she said, "I'll get the pot."

Jessie sat down next to him. There was not much space around the table. As she slid into her chair their arms touched briefly. He didn't know how to give her the parcel. He put it on his lap. He kept his hands under the table. The brown paper was coming loose.

When Mrs. Reever returned from the scullery she said, "I don't know what we would have done without your stove. Honest, I don't." She sat down facing them. She looked at the tablecloth. "You're a real gentleman."

Oxley watched the mother pouring tea and then glanced at Jessie. Jessie was staring at him. She seemed startled for a moment when she met his eyes. Then she smiled. Her eyes never left his face. He held on tightly to the stiff parcel in his lap. He began rubbing his hot palms against the sharp corners beneath the loose brown paper.

He turned his eyes back to the mother. There was a cup of tea before him. "I've been looking forward to meeting you," the mother said, handing a cup of tea to Jessie. "After what our Jessie told us. I mean, you didn't know who she might have been, did you?" She kept her eyes on Jessie when she spoke. She did not pour herself any tea. She smoothed out the tablecloth in front of her several times. Her hand struck against the side of her empty cup and saucer and she jumped. "Would you like more sugar?" she said, her hand poised above her cup. He shook his head and began drinking the tea. It was very strong, almost bitter.

"Have you lived here long?" the mother said. "You don't come from round this part, do you?"

"I come from the country. A country town." He waited. "In Wiltshire."

"It's your work, is it?"

"Yes," he said, "I have to be in London for that."

"Ah, well, everyone's on the move these days, aren't they? I hope you like it up this way. It's not much, though, is it? Maybe they'll do something about it after the war. Is Wiltshire far? I've never been in that area. We'd like to get outside of London ourselves when this lot's over. I thought I was used to the flats, but the war's made everything look different. I'd like to live out at Epping now."

She went to fill up the teapot and Jessie said, "Will you have a sandwich?"

He felt heat rising through his body. He rubbed his hands against the canvas cover of the parachute. He

103

took a sandwich. He tried to avoid her eyes. He glanced around the room for reassurance, as though he might discover something familiar there. The palms of his hands were wet.

Jessie said, "Would you like the window open? The weather's not too bad for this time of year, is it?"

"No, no," he said, "thank you," but she was already up from the table, and his reply was lost in the noise she made pulling the window down from the top.

Mrs. Reever came back with a full teapot and switched on the light as she did so. He looked up with surprise at the sudden illumination and met Jessie's pale eyes. He looked away, toward the crowded mantelpiece: darning wool with a long needle stuck in it, a Coronation mug, a mahogany clock, a picture.

Jessie followed his glance. "My fiancé," she said.

It was a picture of a young man in tropical shorts. He was grinning at the camera, and one of his long socks seemed about to slip down. There was a cloth poppy fixed to the top of the frame.

Jessie sat down again, and for a moment their feet collided beneath the table. He quickly drew his feet under his chair. He struck her thigh with his knee as he did so. He looked at her in panic and edged his chair away. The mother filled up the cups and poured herself some tea for the first time. "Jessie says you don't like the Underground." She bent down beneath the table. "Your brown paper's on the floor." She pulled it out and held it up. It made a loud crackling sound in her hand. He pushed his chair back from the table and scraped the sideboard behind him; he looked down at the stiff canvas parcel. He put his hands on top of it. "I've brought you something," he said, not addressing either of them. He looked up and saw them watching him. "It's a parachute." He handed it in Jessie's direction. "The strings are cut off."

"A parachute?" Mrs. Reever let the brown paper drop.

"It's yellow silk. There's yards of it."

Jessie reached out to take it from him. Their hands touched. He felt his skin against her smooth flesh. He pulled the parachute back into his lap. He began drawing it out of the canvas cover. "It's all silk. Silk panels. You could make clothes—things—with it. People give a lot for them." He felt the silk on his hand. He pulled a corner of the parachute open. "The colored ones, they're for signals, supplies, not for pilots." The corner he had opened tumbled out all over his lap and covered his legs.

Mrs. Reever stood up. "Oh, it's yellow," she said.

Jessie began gathering it together. He felt her hands on his thighs as she reached for the silk.

He pushed himself away from the chair. With a noise like exhaling breath the silk fell in folds beneath the table where he had been sitting.

Jessie picked it up in her arms and cradled it. "Oh, it's lovely," she said, "but why don't you want to keep it?" She held it out to him.

He backed away and fell against the sideboard. A metal tray on top of the sideboard clattered briefly. "I don't need it. You could use it for all sorts of things." He wiped the sweat from his eyes.

"Are you all right?" She dropped the parachute over the back of the chair and made a move toward him.

He edged away from her and stood close to the sideboard. He could feel the metal handle of one of the doors against the inside of his leg.

"Please have a seat," she said. "Wouldn't you like to sit down?"

The parachute fell off the chair. There was silk all

105

over the floor. The air came out of it, and it subsided into a puckered and wrinkled heap under the table.

"It's lovely," she said. "It's very thoughtful of you."

"I have to be off."

"Won't you have some more tea? There's some sandwiches left. You could relax for a few minutes more, if you like."

"Thank you, but I have an appointment."

"Your dad'll be home soon," Mrs. Reever said.

"As long as you're here, would you like to have the spirit lamp?"

"No, not now. I'm not going home now." He moved in the direction of the passageway, avoiding their eyes.

"Very nice to have met you," Mrs. Reever said.

They stood in a knot by the front door.

"That stove," Mrs. Reever said. "It was very kind. I'm sorry you can't take the lamp away with you." She went into the parlor to collect the dirty cups. He heard her rattling them as he stood with Jessie at the front door.

"Come to tea. Tomorrow. Please come. Can you— tomorrow? Half-past five?" He opened the door and looked out into the yard.

"Ta-ta, Mr. Oxley. Thank you," Mrs. Reever called from the parlor.

"All right," Jessie said. "I'd like to."

Thirteen

The next day just after half-past five Oxley led Jessie through the darkness to the big room upstairs.

A few minutes before the appointed time, he left Mrs. Betsie and Mrs. Widdop and went down below to wait for Jessie's arrival. He thought again, as he had so often during the day, of how she had touched him, of her hands reaching across his thighs for the silk when it spilled to the floor.

Above his head one of the women laughed loudly. He was safe with people like that, the Betsies and the Widdops. When he watched their greediness—for a bottle of olive oil, onions, an American fountain pen—and their lovemaking on the carpet upstairs, he didn't think about himself. In the house, in the Cluster Empire, in the streets around the Square during the blackout, he went unnoticed.

He stretched out his hand and felt for the bottles of mustard pickles and chutney, the crate of dried bananas, the boxes of prewar stationery, the chemists' jars, the stack of parachutes. People like the Betsies and the Widdops would keep coming back for the duration. It was something he could rely on.

He heard the knock. He went to the front door without a moment's hesitation.

But when he opened it and caught sight of her smiling at him in the daylight, he felt confused.

"Oh," she said, "you do look better today. I was quite worried about you yesterday." She waited. "If it's not convenient now," she said, "I can always come back another time."

Her eyes seemed paler than ever. He focused beyond her to the spring day outside, to the sun shifting among the weeds in Jubilee Square, and he saw only the dark shape she made in the doorway with the light spilling in around her body. Finally he said, "Please come in. Yes, I'm feeling very good now."

She walked into the house. He closed the door behind her, careful not to let his flesh touch her skin.

She turned to the room off the passageway. She knew her way in the darkness. This afternoon there was no red glow to guide her—only the sweet oily smell of the dried bananas from his room. He caught her by the coat sleeve.

"That parachute," she said. "I've never seen anything like it. The silk. All that yellow silk. I'd like to make you something. I've been thinking of things ever since yesterday."

He could feel her reaching out for the black, crowded wall trying to find the doorjamb. He pulled on her sleeve.

"No, not in there today. Upstairs. I thought we'd have it upstairs today. Here, this way. There's company for tea, a couple of friends. Ladies. They've only just arrived. It's more sociable than downstairs. We can be more at ease."

"What's yours, Mr. Oxley?" a voice sang out as soon as they were inside the big room. "With?"

Jessie stood in the sudden haze of light, unblinking. Oxley's eyes were drawn back to her face as irresistibly as if he were dreaming. He let go of her sleeve.

108

"Take off your coat and make yourself comfortable," he said.

At first she did nothing but stare through the electric glow at the two women.

"Please take off your coat, won't you?" He followed the direction of her eyes: Mrs. Widdop on the divan, wreathed in cigarette smoke, with large artificial pearls beneath her ears; and Mrs. Betsie on the leather chair, wearing a fox pelt across her shoulders, the sharp nose and claw snapped together on her bust; and between the women an oblong fruit crate covered by a lace tablecloth and the tea things set upon it. The cluster of light bulbs on the floor by the fireplace was pointed directly at the women. The light struck upward at their faces, making them look flat and white.

"With?" It was Mrs. Betsie calling to him. "Or without?" She crouched over the tea things, with her arm stretched full out, balancing a lump of sugar at the end of a spoon, which she held above one of the cups. "I've taken over," she said. "I poured while you were downstairs. How do you like it? With or without? I've still to learn."

He turned to the other woman on the divan. "Mrs. Widdop, this is Miss Reever."

"And I'm Mrs. Betsie, dear—Mr. Oxley, my arm's getting numb. With or without?"

He said, "Mrs. Betsie, this is Miss Reever, a new friend of ours from nearby—up along the canal, behind the house. Miss Reever, wouldn't you like to take your coat off and sit down?" Then finally he smiled at Mrs. Betsie, "Without. Thank you. I'll fetch you something to nibble on and fill up the pot."

As he left the room Mrs. Widdop whispered across to her friend, "Maybe you shouldn't have gone ahead and poured, dear. Maybe he likes to do it himself."

109

But all that Mrs. Betsie said in reply was, "Poor chap, eh?" She too spoke in a whisper. The words carried clearly into the room next door. "You're too sensitive, Mrs. Widdop, love. Poor chap," she turned to Jessie. "It's a real tragedy, isn't it, dear?" Her voice rose. "You'll have yours with, won't you? Such a nice man." She began whispering again. "And young really. You don't need too much savvy to see how he broods."

"Well," said Mrs. Widdop, "being shut up in here all day long can't do him much good, can it? Mr. Widdop thinks he's got a pension. I'd say he deserved it, poor fellow. It does seem a shame."

Jessie sat, holding her cup in her lap, on the other leather chair. Her coat was draped over the back of the chair and fell to the floor in heavy dark folds.

Oxley watched them for a few minutes through the warped door.

"Why don't you come over here, dear?" Mrs. Widdop went on. "He likes that place for his tea, I think. And then, besides, I won't have to shout so much."

Without a word Jessie moved across the room, the cup in one hand, the coat in the other.

"Yes, that's better. I know what it's like, if anyone does. My cousin who lives in Glasgow, their boy, he had a terrible accident on his motorcycle. Dragged by a lorry halfway across the street face down. He hasn't been good for much since then. It gives me the willies whenever I think of it, even now. Courting, too, he was. The girl wouldn't have anything to do with him afterward; sent back the ring and all."

In the next room Oxley stood with his hand inside a tin of softening chocolate biscuits, listening to the women. "You can understand her viewpoint, can't you?" Mrs. Widdop said. "Though it wasn't very hot for him, poor chap. Still, what sort of a life would she have

110

had with him that way? He used to sit and cry to himself like a baby all day long. Men don't stop and think what it's like for the woman, though, do they?"

"She wasn't up to much," Jessie said. "No wonder he couldn't take it, with a girl like that." Her voice stung him through the wall. "She couldn't have thought much of him in the first place."

"Yes, it's a nasty business, whatever way you look at it."

"She's to blame."

In the silence that followed, Mrs. Betsie intervened. "You'll be having some more tea when the pot comes back, Miss—er—won't you? How many lumps?"

"I don't hold with the girl's way of thinking," Jessie said. "You've got to take the rough with the smooth."

"You can have all the sugar you want. There's no shortage in this house. It's his friend, Mr. Straker—do you know him? He's got green fingers when it comes to finding things. The stuff grows in his hand."

Before coming back into the big room Oxley rattled the plate against the teapot.

Mrs. Betsie's voice rose as he reappeared. "I was telling Miss—er—"

"Reever," he said.

"That there's no shortage in this house."

Jessie sat on the divan, white in the glare, her fingers on the wrinkled cover. Between her and Mrs. Widdop she had placed her coat in a high heap. Her face, her eyes, were canceled by the electric light. But he saw for the first time the shape of her small body: breasts, thighs, and the slight curve of her stomach. His head began to ache.

Her hands touched his. He reared. Jessie had her hands around the smoking teapot. His stomach muscles contracted with the shock of it. A chocolate biscuit fell to the carpet, face downward. She took the pot from his hands, picked up the biscuit, blew on it, and put it back on the plate. Then she went over to the fruit crate with the pot.

"Oh, just look at those!" Mrs. Betsie said. "See what he had up his sleeve, Mrs. Widdop. I bet your hubby wouldn't mind the sight of those chocolate biscuits, would he?"

"He doesn't smoke and he doesn't drink, but he's a terror for anything sweet."

"My Norman, you know, he thinks the world of him."

"Well, they won't be too long now, will they?" Mrs. Widdop said. "My Reg said he was meeting him at Marble Arch. By the way, Mr. Oxley, how long do you think Freddy Straker's going to be, getting hold of those bananas?"

"You can trust Freddy," he said.

"Oh, we know that, don't we, Mrs. Betsie? That lovely Yank pen he got me for my Reg. If it was anyone else," she closed down her mouth on a chocolate biscuit, "I wouldn't believe you."

"Freddy Straker's a real stick," Mrs. Betsie said to Jessie.

"He's never failed yet," Oxley said.

"I distinctly remember he told us *dried* bananas, though, don't you, Mrs. Widdop? How can you dry a banana? I've never heard of anything like that before. Maybe he's got it mixed up."

"He's not the type, love, is he? Maybe it's something American."

"But they don't grow bananas in America, do they?"

"Well, they're very clever, you have to give them that."

"A bit too clever, if you ask me." Mrs. Betsie sighed.

112

"Like the time—it wasn't more than a month ago—I found a Yank soldier and a bit of skirt in the front garden up against the silver birch. Bold as brass he was, the Yank. Blackout or no blackout, I flashed my torch right on him. 'Haven't you got any shame?' I told him, 'This is private property.' And you know what he had the nerve to turn round and say? 'Well, so's this, lady.' Anybody else would have been off in a flash—even a Pole. So when I saw what was going on I said, 'Well, don't be all night, you two. You'll catch cold out here in the open.' "

"Cheeky lot," Mrs. Widdop agreed. "They do like the girls, though, don't they? My Reg is right, you know. What's decent inside four walls isn't the same outside, is it?"

"He's a fine man. Looks after himself, doesn't he?"

"Well, he doesn't smoke or drink, you see."

"I can't abide a man who doesn't look after himself."

Jessie sat leaning forward, staring down at her feet. Oxley stood against the wall watching her. She had turned her head away from him. She did not try to join in the conversation with the women. Her finger tips were pressed against the divan cover. Every few moments, with a small circular motion, she made an effort to smooth out the resisting creases. At the nape of her neck where her hair had divided and fallen forward toward her face, the light glistened on the downy flesh.

"I've always seen to it that Mr. Widdop eats well."

"It shows." Mrs. Betsie took off her fox, extracting the claw from the pointed mouth, and arranged the pelt carefully on the carpet beside her. "They'll be here shortly."

"Freddy Straker won't be long, either," Oxley said.

Jessie stood up and turned to him. "It must be getting quite dark outside, I should think. I ought to be going now."

113

"No. Not yet," he sprang toward her. But it was all right. There was a noise at the bottom of the stairs. Everybody's eyes turned to the door. It was Freddy coming back. The two women shifted themselves expectantly.

"Hello, hello, hello," he called out on his way up.

And in the small confusion caused by Freddy's return, Oxley put his hand unflinchingly on Jessie's arm. "Please stay for a while. Just a little while, if you like, but don't go yet."

"All right. I will for just a minute or two if I won't be in the way. I didn't tell my mum I'd be late, you see."

"You can't go when Freddy's on his way in, can you?" Oxley said.

"Phew," Freddy said with mock breathlessness. He had a cardboard carton in his arms. "Hello, playmates." He took the carton into the adjoining room.

In a minute he was with them again, holding a square pink box. "When Freddy Straker makes a promise, it's in the bag." He smiled at Jessie. "You're back again, are you, Miss? How are you doing today?"

"Oh, you got the stuff, then?" Mrs. Betsie stood up.

"Look what I brought for you today." He opened the box. It was stationery, tied with green ribbon. "You can't use a beauty like that Yank pen on the notepaper you get these days, can you?"

"Yes, but the pen's not for me," Mrs. Widdop said, sniffing at the box Freddy held right before her nose, "it's for my hubby. Lovely scent it's got, hasn't it?"

"It ought to have. It's genuine Swiss ladies' notepaper. The finest."

"Yes, but it's not for me, you see. He would need men's paper, wouldn't he?"

"It's scented with genuine Midnight in Monte Carlo." Mrs. Betsie inhaled deeply. "Oh, it isn't half sexy."

"See what I mean?" Freddy said to Mrs. Widdop.

"I can tell it's good stuff. Make a beautiful Christmas present, a box of that, wouldn't it? Yes, well I think I'll take it then."

"Do you have any more?" Mrs. Betsie said.

"I'm afraid I can't let you have only one box." Freddy closed the lid and put the box behind his back. "They only come in sets of twelve. It wouldn't be worth our while to let them go one at a time."

"If you don't want them, Mrs. Widdop, love, I'll have them."

"No, maybe I ought to. Seeing that I *do* have the pen."

Mrs. Betsie said, "Those bananas you were trying to get, you did say *dried* bananas, didn't you?"

"They finally arrived. You wait till you see them, ladies."

"I just wanted to make sure that's what you said they were."

"How do they taste?" Mrs. Widdop said.

"Like prewar. Melt in your mouth. No peel on them, either. I'll bring up a sample for you."

As Freddy left the room, Oxley switched off the electric light. The red haze crept upward through the momentary blackness of the change-over. Jessie jerked her head round to where he stood by the light switch. "It's more restful like this," he said to her.

When he looked away he saw a glint of broken glass from under the cupboard door. At the beginning when he walked about in the room, he used to hear the piled-up pieces inside the cupboard shift and settle. But now the glass was packed firm; it was silent even when the couples rolled together on the floor.

Downstairs, Freddy was singing.

"I'll go and put some more water on for the gentlemen. Are you comfy over there, Miss Reever? You can stay for another cup, can't you?"

Mrs. Betsie joined in the refrain of Freddy's song:

> *Keep your eyes on*
> *The bright horizon,*
> *And he'll come back*
> *To you.*

"I love the way Montie Braid sings that," Mrs. Widdop said. "Do you remember him doing 'Señorita, I love you, ay, ay, ay'?"

"He's always good, isn't he?"

Freddy came bounding up the stairs. "Yes, we've got dried bananas," he sang, holding up a full fist before the women. "We've got dried bananas today. Just like pre-war days, eh? Try a nibble off one of these, ladies. There's a banana for each of you, and a couple over. Go on, they won't bite you."

"Here." Oxley took a banana from him and stretched it out toward Jessie; it was as though he were feeding an animal behind bars. She put up her hand, and the red light struck at her engagement ring. Carefully, without touching her, he placed the banana in her grasp. The dark shriveled fruit was slick and oily.

"I'll have this a bit later with my tea, if you don't mind," Jessie said.

"Oh." Mrs. Betsie mashed the end of her banana around in her mouth, "They are funny, aren't they? Taste all right, though, I must say. They feel like dates when you touch them. But with a banana taste."

"Yes, love, they *are* bananas, and no mistake. Whatever will they think of next?"

"Clever—the Yanks," Freddy said. "You can't beat them when it comes to ideas. Anything new and all that. They've got us beat a mile."

116

"Well," said Mrs. Betsie, "they're not really in the war the same way we are, are they? That's why."

"These aren't half bad, are they? Mr. Widdop would love to have some, I know. He doesn't smoke or drink, you see," she said to Jessie.

"They'll be here any minute," Oxley said. "Ready for their tea, I expect."

Mrs. Betsie turned to Jessie. "Are you going steady, dear?"

"No, I'm not." Jessie put the banana in her other hand. "I'll have this with my tea."

Mrs. Betsie took a pencil from her handbag. "How would you like me to settle up with you for some bananas, Mr. Straker? I really wouldn't mind having a few pound. They'd be all right in a trifle or a flan."

Freddy went out to the landing. "I think I can hear the men. Why don't we wait until the gents have had their tea; then we can do it all in a single go." He went down the stairs two at a time, singing to himself.

"He ought to be more careful in the dark. He'll hurt himself one of these days." Mrs. Betsie scratched herself on the thigh with the pencil. "It's my Norman and Mr. Widdop finally, I should hope."

Oxley greeted the men when they appeared in the deep shadow of the door with Freddy: "I'd like you to meet Miss Reever. She's a neighbor of ours."

"This is my hubby, and that's Mr. Widdop," Mrs. Betsie said. "Wherever have you been all this time, Norm? You haven't been encouraging my husband to get up to mischief, have you, Mr. Widdop?"

"You are a scream," Mrs. Widdop said.

Mr. Betsie bent over Jessie. "Haven't I met you before?"

"I don't think so. Where would it have been?"

"No, well perhaps not. I'm always thinking that about

people, aren't I, Winn? You don't mind if I squeeze in between you two on the couch, do you? How are you today, Mrs. Widdop?"

Jessie tried to take her coat away before he sat down, but she was too late. Mr. Betsie moved his eyes over her body. He took hold of her hand and examined it with a surprised expression. "What's that?"

"A dried banana." Jessie looked down at it. "Mr. Oxley's friend, Mr. Straker, got them."

"A what?"

"You heard her, Norm."

"It's a Yank thing," Mrs. Widdop said.

"That's what these are on the side of the plate, then?" Mr. Widdop looked up from the chocolate biscuits. With his forefinger he poked at the two bananas lying beside them. He had drawn up a leather chair and was chewing the biscuits slowly and methodically. He cleaned off his teeth with the tip of his tongue at the end of each mouthful. "I always feel at home here," he said. "How's the tea brewing?" Then he started on the bananas.

Oxley and Freddy went into the kitchen together. Freddy filled up the kettle. Oxley arranged another plateful of biscuits. There were no more chocolate biscuits left; these had pink coconut on top.

"Here," Freddy said. He pulled a handful of brightly wrapped toffees out of an inside pocket of his jacket and scattered them among the biscuits. "Free samples. They'll all have big eyes when they see them. I've got a dozen jars of them coming in next week."

Oxley took one of the toffees and held it in his hand. "The girl," he said, "Jessie, she's nice, don't you think?"

"Yes," Freddy said. "Yes, she is. The quiet sort. But the others"—he whistled softly—"they're a crowd, eh? Believe anything, they would."

"She's different," Oxley said.

118

"Not the buying type, is she? Still, she's not bad—a bit of all right, really," Freddy said. "Smashing legs."

Oxley had been holding the toffee, and he now put it on top of one of the coconut biscuits. The toffee had softened in his hand. He wiped the sweat from his palms against the sides of his trousers, picked up the plate, and went back inside.

As he stepped into the big room Widdop was saying, "Quite good, Marge. Like to try the other, Mr. Betsie? Not really too bad once you get past the look of it."

Oxley saw Betsie shake his head and try to slide a little closer to Jessie. Her coat made it difficult for him. Betsie got up and pushed the coat all the way to the back of the divan. When he sat down again his knees were within striking distance.

"How's the tea, Mr. Oxley?" Mrs. Widdop asked, watching her husband chew.

"Almost ready," Oxley said. "These'll go very nicely with a fresh pot, won't they?"

He held the plate down so that they could see the biscuits and the toffees. He looked around the room. Jessie was not watching him. He took the plate over to the divan and handed it carefully to her. She took it from him and put it in her lap. She sat looking down into the plate.

"Oh," Mrs. Widdop said, "they will be nice, Reg, won't they?"

Oxley said, "I'll see to the pot."

He went out to the black stairwell and felt his way down to his room as quietly as he could. He reached for one of the chemists' jars; he thought of her there upstairs, the light on her neck, her head forward, her eyes down.

When he returned he had a small plump wad at the bottom of his trouser pocket. He had wrapped some pills in a piece of toilet paper.

Freddy was counting bank notes. "You can pick up the fruit and stuff as you go out. I'll have it ready for you by the front door. I might be able to locate a jar or two of toffees for you. They come high, though. It's the sugar."

Drawing her coat up against her side, Jessie shifted toward the end of the divan.

Mrs. Betsie was offering the plate of biscuits and toffees to her husband.

"I'll get the tea," Oxley said.

"Are you cold, Miss?" Betsie asked Jessie.

Oxley brought out a tray of new tea, with extra cups for the men. He had replaced Jessie's cup. The new cup was white with a gold-colored handle. The saucer did not match; it was blue. "Nice and strong, this pot of tea," he said.

"I could do with a nice strong one," Mrs. Widdop said.

Oxley poured from the mantelpiece, keeping his back to the other people in the room. He filled Jessie's cup. He did it slowly and deliberately, but he slopped some of the tea into the saucer, nonetheless. He picked up the saucer carefully and emptied it into the fireplace. Holding it with both hands he carried the tea over to Jessie. He gave it to her.

"Are you having a nice chat?" he said with his eyes on the tea.

"Yes, thank you," she said without looking up.

"Wouldn't you like to try the banana? They're not bad really. It's something new."

Mrs. Betsie put the plate on the floor next to her fur.

120

"Wasn't the traffic shocking today at the Monument?" Widdop asked Betsie.

"It's all the foreigners. I sometimes wonder who it is we're fighting the war for."

Widdop was watching Jessie eat her banana. She was trying to get rid of it as soon as possible. In between quick nibbles at it, she gulped down small mouthfuls of tea, washing the fruit away without tasting more than she had to, like someone swallowing unpleasant medicine.

"Take your time, Miss," Widdop said. "Let your teeth do their proper work, or you'll suffer for it in after years."

"He's got a wonderful digestion," his wife said to everybody there.

Mrs. Betsie stared admiringly at Widdop as he sat on the leather chair with his legs out before him, in complete repose now that Jessie had finished eating. He rested his hands on his belly. He seemed to be waiting for the digestive processes to act on the biscuits, the toffees, the two dried bananas, and the hot tea.

Oxley filled Jessie's cup again without asking her whether she wanted any more. His palms were wet. He stood against the wall, holding the empty teapot and watching her. He kept sliding one hand over the glaze of the teapot, from spout to lid to handle.

Three or four times Jessie opened her eyes as widely as she could; she shook her head each time.

He put the teapot on the mantelpiece and picked up the piece of toilet paper he had left there. It was empty now. He pulled it to shreds with one hand and, still watching Jessie, let the pieces fall into the fireplace among the cigarette ends, the splashes of tea, the food wrappings, the poker and shovel.

Widdop finally drew his legs in. He began to make

121

impatient clicking sounds with his fingernails. Mrs. Betsie closed her eyes and pressed herself farther back into her chair, trailing her hand down to the floor to stroke at the fox pelt. Mrs. Widdop removed her earrings and put them into her handbag. Betsie, his palms resting on his thighs in a casual-seeming way, twitched his knees rhythmically toward Jessie's, as if keeping time to a dance band inside him.

Freddy stood just outside the doorway, pulling his earlobe. Oxley saw that he was watching Jessie. Oxley was still by the mantelpiece.

No one said anything. Now and again the women and their husbands looked sideways at Jessie. All of them seemed to be uncertain about her, even Betsie, twitching his knees, moving steadily closer. Every so often, they looked over at Oxley, as though waiting for a signal. Mrs. Betsie picked out a toffee from the plate by her feet and handed it to her husband. "Have another toffee, Norm dear." Widdop cleared his throat. Betsie leaned over toward his wife, touching Jessie's knee as he did so. "Sweets are good for energy," Widdop said. "Oh," Betsie said quietly when his knee brushed Jessie's. Outside the doorway Freddy smoothed his tie.

And then she keeled over. She fell, without any warning, sideways. Her thighs fell across Betsie, and he jumped as her full weight hit his shoulder. He was still leaning forward with the toffee in his hand. His wife got up quickly from her chair and took the toffee from him. He put his arms around Jessie and laid her back on the divan. She stirred, reached out for help. He held her in his arms. He put his face over hers, lowered it until they almost touched, and then said very softly, "You feeling all right, Miss?" He helped her into a sitting position.

"I feel funny," she said. "All of a sudden." She slid through Betsie's embrace.

122

Betsie tried to lift her head. "Maybe you're tired and need a nice lay-down."

Widdop said, "You've eaten the banana too quickly, you know." He got up and took Jessie's hand. "I expect you're feeling bilious over it. Never abuse your stomach or you'll pay for it. There's nothing wrong with those bananas in themselves."

Oxley had a flask in his hand. He shoved it forward to Betsie, trying not to shake too much as he did so. "Give her this. It's brandy. It'll do her good." He stood over them with his trousers clinging wet to the back of his knees, unable to go any closer, gesticulating. He kept his eyes on Jessie's face. One of her eyelids twitched. He saw the pale lashes move fitfully, flutter up and down; saw her heavy breathing, the way her stomach contracted.

Oxley turned round. "Freddy," he called, "I think she's all right, don't you, Freddy? Her color's fresh enough. She just looks a bit tired. Give her another drop of the brandy. It'll perk her up."

Jessie blinked her eyes at the sting of liquor in her throat. "I feel ever so queer all of a sudden. Queer right through."

"Poor dear." Mrs. Widdop felt Jessie's forehead by reaching over Betsie and touching him as she did so. It's not fever, though."

Oxley said, "She needs a bit of air. It's probably tiredness. Maybe you ought to unbotton her and give her some air."

Freddy came over to the divan. "She ought to lie down."

"Brandy's good," Mrs. Betsie said. She picked up the flask and held it to Jessie's lips. "Have another little drop, dear. Set you up right as rain in a few minutes. There's nothing like it."

Freddy leaned over her. "Can I do anything?" He

123

undid the knot of his tie. He felt her forearm. "Hello," he said. He took off his jacket and laid it carefully on the floor under the divan.

"Norm," Mrs. Betsie said, "why don't you do what Mr. Oxley says and unbutton her collar?"

Betsie reached past Freddy and opened the button at Jessie's throat. He looked up at his wife behind him and said, "All right, Winn?"

"Yes, go on, love."

"Yes, well, I will."

Freddy stepped out of his way.

Mrs. Betsie turned to Oxley. "Is it Three-Star, Mr. Oxley?" she said.

Betsie opened Jessie's blouse, revealing the white straps of her slip and brassière. He peered down at her and then began to rummage his way through her under-clothing toward her breasts as if feeling for soap in the bath.

Every so often he turned round to look at his wife. She smiled at him for a moment each time he did so. She watched him intently, and while she watched she undid —discreetly, unobtrusively, as though she did not want to lag behind—the zipper of her own dress.

"That's the way," Oxley said to Betsie.

Widdop was out of his chair, his jacket left neatly folded on the seat, holding himself by the stomach and pushing past Oxley to help the others.

Widdop knelt down beside Jessie and lifted her hand as if to take her pulse.

Freddy stood watching Betsie undo the straps of her brassière. He leaned forward and touched her cheek. "She looks much better already," he said.

She had opened her eyes and was breathing regularly again. Widdop let go of her hand. She moved her hands up and down a couple of times, as though she were try-ing to reach for something.

Oxley said to Freddy, "She's looking much better, isn't she?"

Freddy pushed Widdop to one side. He put his hands on her legs very gently, and let them rest there. He looked round at Oxley. Oxley began to back away from them. Freddy moved his hands to and fro across her legs and then reached up beneath her skirt and pulled her stockings down. With both hands he felt along her bare legs. His fingers began to move rapidly, nervously. He undid the fasteners at the side of her skirt.

She closed her eyes. Silently she began to cry.

Widdop tried to get past Freddy. Freddy elbowed him out of the way and bunched up Jessie's coat. He felt the pocket and pulled out something wrapped in newspaper. He threw it on the floor. Then he bunched up the coat again and placed it under her head.

"There, there," Freddy said, putting the back of his hand up to her cheeks and trying to brush the tears away. "You're all right, aren't you? There, there." He pressed himself hard against the side of the divan and stroked her cheek.

Oxley said, "She just needs to relax."

The two women turned as he walked past them on his way out of the room.

Through the cracked door he could see Jessie's face and the tears falling slowly into her ears and her hair. Her hands were still. Her body was completely relaxed. She did not seem to be aware of what was going on around her, to know that her skirt and knickers and stockings were down at her ankles and her slip up around her neck, as if she had been bound with her own clothing. He saw Freddy push the other men back from the divan, and how the women, having stripped themselves almost naked, waited: Mrs. Widdop holding her dress in front of her, Mrs. Betsie pressing her palms against the steel snapper of her fox.

Jessie had stopped crying. Her eyes were open again. Freddy got up from the floor and sat on the edge of the divan. He reached for the top of his belt. "There's a good girl," he said. With his hands on his belt buckle he kissed her on the mouth and the neck and the ear. He undid his belt and put his arms around her. "There's a good girl," he said several times. Mrs. Betsie fell from her chair to the floor beside Widdop, pulling at his legs and rubbing her breasts against his calves, until, as on the nights before, swearing and calling her husband's name, she and the other woman's husband rolled over together. No one took any notice when the sirens went and the sky outside became alive. Betsie and Mrs. Widdop lay by the fireplace, the other couple below the divan. Oxley watched their movements, heard their words, their soft cries, their moans of affection, found himself unable, finally, to see anything but Jessie Reever: unconscious on the divan, the light on her soft, downy thighs, farther than he from what was going on. He could not take his eyes from her. He was condemned to watch to the end, to see her beneath Freddy, who, every moment, was driven to further excitement, to roughness, by the sound of Mrs. Betsie, on the floor with the other woman's husband, cursing her way to relief.

Fourteen

They began to look for their clothing.

Freddy got off the divan and reached for his trousers. He had thrown them on the floor by the divan. As he lifted his trousers a lighter fell from one of the pockets and struck the parcel he had taken from Jessie's coat. He bent down for the lighter and rubbed it against his shirt-tail. He looked at Jessie. He returned the lighter to his trouser pocket and held the back of his hand against her neck for a moment. With his knuckles he gently touched the place below her ear. After a few seconds more he bundled his clothing in his arms and went through the door at the far end of the room, into the lavatory.

"She's out like a light."

Mrs. Widdop was the first of them to speak.

"Reg," she said, "what do you think of her? Feel her forehead. It's very clammy."

She spoke quietly, as if afraid of waking the girl.

"What's the matter, Marge?" Widdop said.

Betsie took a handkerchief from the inside pocket of his jacket, unfolded it, and handed it across the room to Mrs. Betsie. "How long ago was the All Clear, Winn? Maybe half an hour? Did you hear it when it went?"

Freddy was whistling softly behind the lavatory door.

"About half an hour," Mrs. Betsie said.

Widdop put on his jacket and went to the divan. "The

stomach," he said, looking down at the girl, "it's a dangerous thing to mess around with. Is there any of that brandy left?"

"No, there isn't. Perhaps we ought to get her another drop." Mrs. Widdop felt Jessie's brow again, stroking the hair away from the girl's face as she did so. "Maybe it's a nice cup of tea she needs more than the brandy."

Mrs. Betsie folded up the handkerchief and put it in her handbag. She walked over to Mrs. Widdop. She peered at Jessie. "Brandy's best, though, Mrs. Widdop, love. There's bound to be some more downstairs, isn't there?" She looked over toward the lavatory door. "I hope Freddy Straker's not going to be long inside there." She smoothed down her dress and touched Jessie's temples. "Oh, you're right. She does feel clammy."

"Reg," Mrs. Widdop said, "come over here and have a feel of her forehead." She rearranged the coat beneath Jessie's head.

Widdop placed one palm on Jessie's brow. Then he held her wrist and looked at his watch. "She seems all right to me, Marge, really she does. She's been overdoing it, I suppose. Poor girl, though. I expect she'll have cramps when she wakes up."

They stood around the girl, adjusting their clothes, putting themselves in order.

Mrs. Betsie began combing out her hair. "Norm, dear, are you nearly ready? I'll run down and ask Mr. Oxley for some more of that brandy for her, shall I? Then we can get off home and have something warm." She touched his arm.

Mrs. Widdop said, "Don't bring him up yet, eh? Not with the girl like this. Why don't you give me a hand with her first?"

The women began straightening Jessie's clothes. Jessie did not move at all as, working together, one of them

128

lifting her slightly and the other pulling at her clothes, they fastened her brassière, eased the slip down over her body, drew up her knickers.

Mrs. Widdop began to whisper. "Look at this poor thing's neck, Mrs. Betsie. She'll show that mark for a week, I should think. He's a very passionate lad with his kissing, isn't he? I never thought he had the interest."

"He's a deep one, and no mistake. Still"—Mrs. Betsie examined the girl—"it's nearly on the shoulder. It won't really notice."

Widdop sat on a leather chair. "Marge, will you be long? Is the girl all right?"

"I won't be more than another minute or two. Mrs. Betsie, you've got her other stocking, have you? This one's laddered something terrible."

Mrs. Betsie squinted at the stocking in her hand. "She won't have much wear out of them now. Never mind, though. Freddy Straker should be able to fix her up with anything she needs, shouldn't he? He seems to have taken a real fancy to her." She eased Jessie's toes into the stocking. "Throw us the other one, Mrs. Widdop. Have you got her skirt?"

"Winn," Mr. Betsie said softly, looking toward the lavatory door, "do you think he could get petrol coupons? That's what I'd really like."

Mrs. Widdop fastened Jessie's skirt. "She feels warmer. She looks quite nice now."

Mrs. Betsie put her arm around her husband. "Petrol coupons? I don't see why not. I'll go and get the master of the house as soon as the lav is clear. What's he doing in there all this time, I'd like to know."

Mrs. Widdop said, "Some men are like that with the lav. They're worse than women."

"Shall I ask him about the petrol coupons, Norm, or will you?"

129

"You do it, Winn. He's a ladies' man, isn't he?"

Mrs. Widdop bent over Jessie again and straightened the seams of her stockings. "She looks a lot better, doesn't she? Stay here, Mrs. Betsie, love, and I'll go down myself and get a drop more brandy from Mr. Oxley. Hark at Freddy whistling in there."

Mrs. Widdop took a comb out of her handbag. She began combing the damp hair off Jessie's face. She tried to wave the ends of it between her fingers, but the girl's hair stayed straight. "I'll get the brandy. The poor thing had better have something." She put her comb away, stopped, opened her handbag again and took out a bottle of scent. She tilted the bottle onto her fingertips and dabbed them behind Jessie's ears. Then she walked toward the door.

Oxley moved. Only when he realized that Mrs. Widdop was coming for him did he take his eyes off Jessie: laid out neatly; dressed again; beginning now to stir; ready to come back to consciousness. For a second he watched Jessie move her legs, shift her arms, take a deep, uncontrolled breath. Then, as the woman came toward him, he pulled himself away from the door. He tried to get down the stairs as quickly as he could without making any noise. His body was numb from having been pressed hard against the doorjamb. His face was sore where he had held it to the crack in the wood.

The door opened at the top of the stairs.

He stopped in the hallway, holding his breath. He heard Mrs. Widdop's shoes advance to the edge of the landing, the creak of the banisters as she leaned against them, and then her voice above him.

"Mr. Oxley." She waited. "Mr. Oxley. We're about ready now, Mr. Oxley. Can you hear me down there? It's your friend, Miss—"

And while she paused to remember the name, he

made a noise, a furtive movement on the floor and against the wall, as he tried to get back in his room.

"Oh."

Up above him in the blackness she sounded surprised.

"Mr. Oxley? You're there, then, Mr. Oxley, are you? Mr. Oxley, is that you?"

He was standing by the door of his room. He tried to sound natural, calling back to her.

"You're ready to go? I thought it might be about the time. I heard you moving around up there."

"Your friend's a little down in the mouth. She's still a bit faint. I wondered if there's a drop more brandy left for her. She needs something."

"Oh, yes. I'll bring some up with me directly. Nothing bad, is it?"

"Passed out, poor thing."

On his way up to the big room with the brandy in his hands he heard Mrs. Widdop whispering to the others.

"It gave me a bit of a turn," she was saying.

Mrs. Betsie said, "I sometimes wonder what he gets up to here all alone in a place like this."

Freddy brushed past Oxley in the doorway. "I'll get their stuff ready downstairs. They're all set to take off."

"Lovely," Oxley said, avoiding his glance, seeing instead the girl lying on the divan, with her eyes open, staring fixedly up at the ceiling, breathing deeply. He went halfway across the room and stopped. "Mrs. Widdop, would you like to give her a little of this?"

"Thank you. She's much warmer already. She'll be herself in a minute or two. Ah, there you are, my girl." Mrs. Widdop tried to beckon Oxley over to the divan. "Feeling better, dear? You've been overdoing it recently, haven't you?"

Mrs. Betsie came back into the room. She arranged

the fox around her shoulders. She pointed to the door behind her. "Want to use it, Norm, before we start off home? Oh, hello, Mr. Oxley."

"Take care of your stomach"—Widdop shook his head at Jessie—"and your stomach'll take care of you. That's always been my motto, hasn't it, Marge? Well, good night, all. And good night, Miss. Nice to have met you."

"That's better, Miss," his wife said encouragingly as they left.

"Norm?"

"Ready."

They both smiled at Jessie.

Her eyes were open, but she looked at no one.

Mr. Betsie said, "We'll be seeing you here again in the week, I expect. Look after yourself, anyway, Miss, and bye-bye for now. Good night, Mr. Oxley. Freddy's got our stuff downstairs, has he?"

And then Oxley was alone with Jessie.

He took a step away from her. She moved her elbows. She opened and closed her mouth several times. Soft, incomprehensible noises came from the back of her throat. She seemed to be forming words beyond his hearing. He raised his hands to his neck and his ears. She started to cry. He watched her breasts heave and her stomach shake with the effort of tears. But after a few seconds she stopped. Very slowly she touched her thighs and felt the lower part of her stomach. Every few seconds she shifted her weight. After a while she lay still, with her hands clenched upon her middle.

He meant to say something to her. His mind went blank. He watched how she rammed both her fists hard into the base of her stomach. She had drawn up her knees a little way.

132

He started to go outside to make her some tea, but then he remembered about the tea and he turned back in her direction. She was staring at him from the divan. She lay flat out. Her head was twisted round toward him. Her lips were the color of sand. She stared at him without blinking. She said, "What time is it?"

He said, "Can I get something for you? Can I get an aspirin for you?"

She shook her head very slowly, very deliberately, as if she were signaling to somebody a long way off.

"You had a nasty turn." He looked down at his hands while he spoke. He placed one hand inside the other and pressed them together until they hurt. "You're all right now, aren't you?"

"What time is it please?" she said, staring at him. Her voice was low and expressionless.

"It must be about nine o'clock now. The All Clear went a while ago. Would you like some water?"

She shook her head.

"Let me get something for you, please."

She began to cry again, sobbing now, shaking all over. Her head rocked from side to side, her shoulders moved, and then her stomach and thighs and feet, as if feeling were coming back into her entire body. She clutched at her elbows, crossing her arms over her breasts.

He put his hand out to her. He went to the divan. Violently she pushed herself toward the wall. When she was as far from him as possible she turned to look at him. Her mouth opened and closed, but no sound came out.

His hand hung in the air above the divan. "Couldn't I get something for you?" he said.

"What's happened to me?" She passed her tongue across her lips. "How long was I out? What's happened? All the others have left."

"Nothing. They've gone home. You're all right here. Lie still for a minute while I get you an aspirin. You'll feel more like yourself in a little while."

"I don't want anything. I want to go home."

She tried to sit up. She used the wall for support and pushed herself against it. She raised her head. Then she fell back on her coat. After a minute or two of stillness she turned to the wall and began pulling at her stomach as if she were in pain and could tear it from her. "It hurts," she said, "it hurts. What's been going on? What have you been doing to me?"

"Nothing," he said, "I've done nothing." He walked away from the divan to the fireplace. "Wait till you feel a little better." Involuntarily he struck his hand hard against the side of the mantelpiece.

He watched her back heave as she pulled at herself. She was crying again. He could not take his eyes from her; he saw where her hair had parted and revealed her downy neck.

When the sobbing left her she went limp. She turned over and lay staring up at the ceiling with her hands clenched tight over her stomach. Her face was wet and fevered.

He could hear Freddy downstairs. He listened to him say "Good night" to the last of the visitors.

"Why did you do it?" she said.

Painfully, sobbing again, she managed to prop herself up against the wall. She eased her feet over the edge of the divan, stretched them toward the floor.

He went to the divan and tried to help her. She tore at him.

"I'm all right. Leave me be. I don't want any more of it." She stared down at her torn stockings. "Why did you have to do it like this?"

"You're all right. I didn't do anything. That's the truth. Let me get you something before you go."

134

"I don't want anything from you. Get away from me."

For a while she sat on the edge of the divan, looking down at her ankles, at her laddered stockings. Gradually she seemed to gather strength, but when she got up from the divan she looked very pale and slight, and for a minute or two she was uncertain on her feet. Then she straightened her back. She smoothed out her skirt and tucked her blouse into it. She pushed her hair from her eyes. There was a button missing from the front of her blouse. Her brassière showed white where her blouse did not come together. With one hand she held the gap closed and with the other she picked up her coat from the divan. It was rumpled and badly creased. She shook it out and the effort seemed to exhaust her. She waited for a moment. She put her coat on and did it up. She held a hand to her brow and looked back at the divan. Then she walked toward the door. Halfway across the room she suddenly stopped and put her hands into her coat pockets, as if she had forgotten something. She felt around in her pockets. Again she looked back.

She said, "You've taken the spirit lamp, have you? You can keep it. Good-bye."

He heard her groping her way down the stairs. The room was unnaturally still. He looked around at the dirty cups, the puckered carpet, the creased cover of the divan. On the floor by the side of the divan he saw the parcel that contained the spirit lamp and next to it one of Mrs. Widdop's large pearl earrings. He ran down the stairs after her, lost his footing at the bottom, and fell against the hall table. He knocked the glass dome with his elbow, heard it shatter on the wall beside him. He felt the stuffed weasel roll against his foot.

There was a voice beside him. "Anything up, mate?"

"She's hurt. We've hurt her."

"Well, it's only her neck. It'll be gone in a day. I get carried away sometimes."

135

"She's hurt."

Freddy sounded defensive. "It wasn't the first time she's had it, you know. Is she trying to say it was the first time?"

And then he was outside in the damp night air with the mist on his face, stumbling over the smashed brick and running round the back of the house to the canal.

She was just in front of him when he made her out in the night. She was standing right on the edge of the embankment with her arms folded around her middle. She half turned when she heard him behind her. He caught a glimpse of her distraught expression before she began to run, sobbing wildly, away from him and the house and the lamplight, toward the iron bridge and the other side of the canal where she belonged. He ran toward her as she fell crying to the grass. He helped her up, felt her body again before she pulled herself away.

"Leave me alone, do you hear? Haven't you had enough out of me already?"

"I just want to help you," he said.

"You're the one who needs help. Why did you do it like that? You didn't even think about it, did you? What it means to the other person? You just wanted to take a liberty. It could have been anybody as far as you was concerned. Doesn't make any difference to you, does it? People are all the same to you."

"You've had a shock," he said. "I didn't do anything. You're different from them." He put his hands out toward her. "I was frightened. I saw you were sorry for me."

She started to weep. "Look what you did," she said. She walked to the bottom of the bridge. "All you wanted was to take a liberty. You didn't want anything else. You couldn't see there was anything else. Sorry for you? Yes, I am."

He ran towards her. "Don't go away," he said, unable to see her clearly in the mist. "Please don't go now. I didn't want to hurt you."

"Don't you come another step," she cried as she went. "Not a single step further. You're no good."

Halfway across the bridge she called down to him again. "There wasn't any need to have done what you did." There was no anger or fear in her voice now. "Not that way, there wasn't."

Fifteen

The next afternoon he waited by the brick pillars. After a while a door slammed on the ground floor, and there they were: three of them, silent, walking into the darkening rain with bundles under their arms, the mother in front of her, the father behind. As they turned to go through the other end of the yard he caught a glimpse of her face—white and tired above the colored scarf she wore tightly knotted around her neck—saw her shake her head when her father spoke, then touch the ends of her uncovered damp hair. He had to bite down on his tongue to stop himself from calling out her name. There was something he needed to say to her. He had to get close enough to tell her. Then the sirens blew. They began to run, Jessie, the father, the mother.

People suddenly came rushing out of the flats.

"Quick, Phil."

Doors slammed all over the building.

From a high window a green blanket descended, opened in the air, sailed sideways to the yard, lay wet on the ground.

Men, women, charged about, filled the space between him and Jessie.

He went to follow her. A big, breathless man smelling of food knocked him hard against the wall. He fell against his shoulder; his knee went under.

"Where's Florrie?"

"Lou, what's up?"

A door opened beside him. On the front step a woman stood weeping. "Jack, come on."

"I'm staying put, just like I said."

The woman darted in front of Oxley. "Sod you then! Sod you! Do you hear me?"

From inside the flat the man shouted after her, "Just like the rest of your bleeding side! You're all yellow!" and slammed the door.

An old man gathered the green blanket into his arms and then shouted upward, "Turn off the gas before you come!"

Oxley held his paining knee against the wall. Blood was trickling down his arm. People ran past him, pushing and shouting.

Then the sirens stopped, and he heard a voice say quietly, "You remembered the salt?"

Oxley caught at somebody going by. "Which way's the underground from here?"

"Follow us, mate. First right, second left on Mafeking Road"—the man's voice got fainter and fainter—"turn left again, and it's straight in front of you. It's not far, mate. Follow us." But by then they were gone into the dark with the others.

The guns opened up without any warning. In the headlong streak of light, he saw slanting rain, tram lines flaring into the distance, then the name plate, "Mafeking Road." A smell of ammonia from a public lavatory stung his nostrils. A car without lights bumped along close to the curb and turned off ahead. His hands slipped against a shop window, and he fell into a man's outstretched arms.

"Watch your step, there."

It was a warden standing on the corner; the white

helmet was just visible. "Here, hop it. God knows what's coming over tonight. First they said it's the flying minnies—now the bloody guns is going off. Go on, hop it—take cover."

"I want the Underground."

"That's right. It's no more than three minutes from here. Left and left. Go on, now—hop it. Keep left."

He stumbled on. There seemed to be nobody else in the street. He looked up. For a moment it seemed as though the sky was splitting open. A jagged stretch of rooftops—cornices, chimney stacks, a huge cut-out bottle of whisky in an advertisement—burst into sharp, black relief against a blaze of yellow light. Glass fell into the road—a roar like water, then an endlessly repeated tinkle on every side. Slivers, flakes, dropped round him in the rain. He put his hands before his face. They fled upward to cover him without his realizing it.

Down below he saw lights.

A man was smoking at the foot of the turned-off escalator of the Underground station. He took the pipe out of his mouth and said, "Where'd it hit, mate? It sounded bloody near to me. I was halfway down the stairs and—wallop!" He kept raising his eyes in the direction of the street. He stopped. "You feeling all right? D'you need a handkerchief or something, mate?"

Oxley shook his head. There were voices not far away. The girl was somewhere within, he knew—on the platform, past the corner ahead of him.

The man drew circles in the air with his pipe.

"The rocket?" Oxley said, "Not far." He walked away.

At the corner he put out a hand to steady himself. The walls curved up and around him. The station began to rock. A poster said: "Louise, Dressmaker and Renova-

140

tor." He saw that his hands against the wall were cut all over. He brushed a tiny piece of glass from his knuckle and watched the bead form, slowly swell, break wet across the skin. His hands trembled on the shaking wall; lights splashed across his face; beyond the corner a train drew in. A harsh voice shouted in his ear. "You all right, chum?" The man was beside him again. The train stopped, and he heard the sound of doors opening.

"A first-aid helper—that's what you need," the man shouted. "You got caught in it upstairs, didn't you? There's always a first-aid helper along the platform. I'll take you there, mate. Hold on."

Lights charged over him again. He swayed. The man caught him by the arms. The pipe dropped to the ground.

"No," Oxley said, "I fell—in the road—I'm all right."

"Can't hear you, mate. The train—"

"Let go."

"Come on, chum, you don't have to try and be a hero to me. I was in the trenches in the first one. I know how you feel."

He couldn't get himself from the man's grasp. "I'll be all right in a minute. Let me catch my breath."

"You're all done up. Let's go and get your hands seen to, eh? Come on, like a good fellow."

"Let me alone." Turning from the man, he knocked one of his hands against the wall. Blood spurted across his knuckles and wrist.

The man let go and backed away quickly. With his eyes fixed on Oxley he squatted down and felt along the ground for his pipe. The stem was broken. The man waved his broken pipe at him. One of his eyelids twitched, out of control. "You're a bloody idiot, you are."

Oxley took the corner.

People sat under bright posters all the way along the curving wall. Some of them stood chatting. Two girls with arms linked walked along the edge of the platform. All the iron bunks seemed to be claimed.

Halfway down the platform he stepped into a recess in the wall by the emergency stairs. He couldn't see her or the parents among the shelterers nearby. His eyes moved farther along the platform.

"How you feeling, chum?"

The man was back, still carrying the broken pipe, as if he didn't know what to do with the pieces. Still twitching, he stared at Oxley, slightly hesitant when he spoke: "Don't you want to get your hands seen to? You don't want to let the germs get in there, do you?"

Oxley put his hands against the wall behind him, hid them under the skirts of his raincoat. His body felt numb. He heard a child's insistent voice saying, "Chocolates, Mummy, chocolates!" Pressing himself back against the tiles, he looked along the platform for Jessie and her parents. He put his hand up to his face and closed his eyes.

"Hold up, young fellow," the man's voice said into his ear. "I'll take you. It's not far."

Only Oxley's mouth moved. "Leave me be, please," he said and went off by himself to find the girl.

But when he saw them a few yards ahead of him, he stopped. The three of them sat against the wall on a narrow strip of rush matting. Jessie was in the middle, hugging a cushion to her breast. They seemed to be talking quietly, steadily. He watched their lips move. He felt a cramp in his arms. None of them was looking in his direction. He didn't know how he could go and speak to her.

At his side there was a space between the shelterers. He sat down quickly, drew up his knees, and made him-

142

self as small as possible. By leaning his head slightly forward, by letting it rest on his knees, he could watch the girl and her parents.

"Mrs. Lomax"—the woman next to him got up—"I feel a bit funny. Come and see what's going on by the ticket office."

The space to his right was empty. He pulled his legs in parallel to the wall and stretched them out. He never took his eyes off the girl. Jessie's chin was on the cushion. She rocked herself from side to side while she spoke to her parents. Her father unwrapped a sweet, put it in his palm, and handed it across to her mother. Jessie shook her head.

"Excuse me—mind moving your legs? Move them out in front of you, eh?" A man, a woman and a boy, holding carrier bags, squashed themselves in. "All right, now," the man said to the boy, "what's the capital of Australia?"

"Leave the boy alone," the woman said. She was next to Oxley, and he felt the warmth of her body.

"He's got to learn, hasn't he?"

Oxley knocked over one of their carrier bags when he got up.

"Watch out where you're going, mister."

Oxley saw them staring at his hands as he fumbled with the bag.

Jessie was looking down into the cushion. A couple of feet away from her he waited for a moment, burning and dry, trying to moisten his mouth with saliva. Then he went to her.

"That's him, that's him," a familiar voice said. People came running along the platform. Jessie looked up. It was as though he had struck her. The cushion went out of shape, became smaller against her breast. Her knuckles were white with the pressure. He saw her ring

143

glint. She put the cushion up to her face and dropped her head into her father's arms.

"Jessie—" Oxley said hopelessly.

"That's him, that's the geezer."

The father looked up at Oxley in surprise.

A man in a black uniform with a white star on his breast, and a W.V.S. woman dressed in green took Oxley by the shoulders.

"He got caught in it in the street. See the blood?" The man was still holding the pieces of pipe.

Jessie's back shook.

The father stroked her hair with his large stiff hands. "Here—what's going on?"

"Jessie"—the mother tried to raise herself—"what is it?" The mother recognized him. "Oh, it's you. Is anything wrong?" She tried to get up, but Oxley was right in front of her with the others holding him, and there wasn't enough room. She half-stood there, her back curved against the station wall.

"Who is it?" the father said to the mother. He stroked a handful of Jessie's pale hair.

The man said, "He's hurt himself. I knew that straight off. See his hands?"

The mother said, "Dad, what's wrong with our Jessie? Jessie, what's wrong?"

Oxley spoke to the girl's shivering back. "There's something I need to make clear."

"He's got shell shock. Come with us and have your hands bandaged."

"It wasn't me," he said to Jessie.

They tried to take him away with them, but he did not move. "I was outside all the time. I wanted to tell you that. It wasn't me in the room with you."

The first-aid man pulled Oxley gently by the elbow. "Something wrong with your hands, is there? Let's have a look at them, shall we?"

144

He put his hands inside his pockets. "It was the others, you see. Freddy and the others."

"What do you want with our Jessie?" the mother said.

The father lifted Jessie's head. "Do you know this bloke?"

People began drifting toward them. "What's all the fuss?" someone said.

The W.V.S. woman slipped her arms around his waist, above the reddening pockets. "Why don't you come with us and have a nice rest?"

"You see, I was outside all the time."

People along the platform were staring. They started to crowd in. "What's happening, Ron?" a woman said.

The first-aid man was beginning to lose his temper. "You don't want to give these people any trouble, do you?"

"Jessie, who is he?" her father asked. "What does he want with you?"

"It wasn't me in the room."

The man with the pipe started to clear a circle. "Don't crowd him, now. He's caught a shock up in the raid. Give him some space."

"You see what the difference is?" Oxley said.

"What the hell do you want with our Jessie?"

A child ran against his legs, giggling.

"Come here!" a woman screamed.

"Don't you see? It was Freddy."

"If you don't calm down a bit and come along with us, I'll have to use force. It's my duty to the public. You're causing a disturbance down here."

"Jessie, don't you see the difference?"

She lifted her head. He saw the wet, streaked face; the lips trembling, pale; the words forming in pain. "I don't understand," she said.

145

The father clambered to his feet. "What the bleeding hell have you done to her?"

People pushed in farther.

"Let him alone, he's suffering from shock."

Oxley watched her turn to her mother, saw her shake with sobbing. She lay hunched over against her mother's arm.

He tried to lean forward and touch her. "I only watched," he said. "That's all I did. I only watched!"

She lifted her head. He saw the pain in her face, the mouth open as if she had stopped breathing, her eyes full on him.

"Come with us, or I'll have to use my discretion with you."

"Jessie girl, what's he on about?" The father snatched him by the raincoat.

The man with the pipe pushed between. "He's hurt. Can't you see? Let him go, the poor sod."

Hands reached for him. The W.V.S. woman let go and others moved in. Jessie's face seemed frozen. She stared at him as if she could not look away. He turned from her. He pulled himself free and started to run. Voices rose around him. He ran along the platform, into a recess, reached for the iron banister and dragged himself up the emergency stairs, round and round, upward into the street without stopping, dizzy against the curving iron, while footsteps charged behind him, then died away, and only a solitary voice was left shouting hoarsely from far below, "Come back. You're hurt. Come back."

The rain struck down at his hands; he didn't feel it anywhere else. Glass crunched beneath his feet. The girl's expression was before his eyes. He slipped and fell into a puddle full of glass with his hands splayed out before him. Hardly knowing the way, he twisted on to-

146

ward the canal, the Square, the house. Somewhere a whistle blew. The black sky shook violently, and the sound of an explosion lurched at him with a great gust of warm, soft wind around it. He reached out for walls, doors, lampposts—anything solid, firm enough to push himself away from and keep him going—ran blindly into the windscreen of a car abandoned in the middle of the road. There were flames ahead. He ran headlong down to the back gardens and the iron bridge, thinking only of the girl and what he had done to her. He wanted to get inside the house, to close the door behind him and never come out again. The light around him wavered. He saw grass under his feet. The canal, the bridge, the houses were red. Mrs. Clatley's house suddenly rose into view on the other bank, flickering with light. While he watched, a huge piece of its roofing felt shot up into the air and turned to ash. As the sparks subsided and then the smoke, the light died away. Before the Square went completely dark again, he saw that there was nothing left to reclaim.